Just a Bit Wrong

(Straight Guys Book 4)

Alessandra Hazard

Table of Contents

Chapter 1 6

Chapter 2 24

Chapter 3 41

Chapter 4 49

Chapter 5 59

Chapter 6 67

Chapter 7 70

Chapter 8 74

Chapter 9 81

Chapter 10 91

Chapter 11 97

Chapter 12 105

Chapter 13 116

Chapter 14 123

Chapter 15...135

Chapter 16...140

Chapter 17...145

Chapter 18...151

Chapter 19...160

Chapter 20...171

Chapter 21...178

Chapter 22...185

Chapter 23...195

Chapter 24...202

Chapter 25...207

Chapter 26...211

Chapter 27...216

Epilogue..226

About the Author 233

Just a Bit Wrong

Chapter 1

Tristan DuVal wasn't in a good mood. "I still don't understand why I can't get a physiotherapist I know. I don't know that guy."

The look his personal assistant shot him was long-suffering at best. "Because the club's physiotherapists are overworked already," she said. "And Dr. Sheldon wants you to work with a therapist he trusts."

Tristan checked the time on his phone. "The guy is late. I don't have all day."

He turned his face away to hide his smile when Lydia gritted her teeth. However, her voice was remarkably calm as she said, "He's only seven minutes late, Tristan. And it's the third time you've said that in the last five minutes."

Tristan gave her an innocent look. "But he's late!"

"You're late all the time, princess," Lydia muttered under her breath, which was clearly not meant for his ears. Despite being his personal assistant for over a year, Lydia still had no idea how sharp his hearing was and had the habit of saying nasty things about him when she thought he couldn't hear. It was pretty amusing.

Tristan suppressed a smile. He knew he should probably stop deliberately exasperating her, but he was so bored. Now that he was injured and pretty much confined to the house, winding up his personal assistant was the only remotely interesting thing to do. It was almost fun to watch Lydia try to hold back smartass comments she wanted to make. Almost.

"Zach Hardaway comes highly recommended," Lydia said louder. "I'm sure there's a good reason for his tardiness. He's an outrageously expensive physiotherapist and personal trainer. He must be good."

Tristan shrugged. His team doctor promised to find him the best physiotherapist to help him recover from his groin injury, but Tristan hadn't asked for any details; that was Lydia's job. "What good does it do for me if he isn't here? My injury isn't going to heal itself. I'm tired of waiting."

"Then let's go back inside," Lydia said, a note of exasperation creeping into her voice again. "I'm pretty sure you aren't supposed to be walking anyway."

Leaning back against the tree, Tristan looked at the house and scowled. "I'm sick of being stuck inside all day. I'm not an invalid." This time he wasn't complaining just to annoy Lydia. The lack of activity really had been driving him crazy. He missed football. Missed the feeling of being healthy and fit, the wind in his face as he sprinted toward the goal, the elation he felt when he scored, the roar of the crowd singing and chanting his name. Football was his life. The only thing that mattered.

Tristan looked at the gray sky. It was March already. The World Cup was just three months away. Time was running out. He needed to return to the pitch as soon as possible and regain his form if he wanted to impress the National Team's coach. Tristan might be the most talented English player in generations (in his humble opinion), but he had relatively little experience on an international level and he knew that hindered his chances of being chosen. The coach was rather old-fashioned and preferred trusted veterans to young rising stars. And now his injury had only complicated everything.

The longer he stayed injured, the less his chances were of participating in the World Cup. And to make matters worse, it was March and he still didn't have a physiotherapist—or rather, his physiotherapist had apparently decided he had better things to do than his fucking job.

Tristan shifted his gaze back to Lydia. "Call Dr. Sheldon and ask him where that useless idiot is."

Behind him, someone cleared their throat. "That won't be necessary," said a dry voice. "The useless idiot is here."

Tristan grimaced. Awkward. And a little inconvenient. He liked making a good first impression on people. He had a public image to maintain, after all.

Fixing a smile on his face, Tristan turned around.

His smile faded a little and he moistened his lips with the tip of his tongue.

The man who stood a few feet away—Zach Hardaway—*wasn't* the most handsome man he'd ever seen.

He wasn't. But he exuded such confidence, strength and virility that he gave the impression of being incredibly handsome. He was tall, with a firmly muscled body and broad shoulders. His thick brown hair had golden gleams in it. He had a strong jaw, lean cheeks, olive skin, and a pair of steely gray eyes. His mouth was finely molded with a slight wry quality to it, but it didn't soften the hardness of his features at all. There was a furrow between the guy's brows as he studied Tristan.

"You're favoring one leg," he said. "Go inside."

Tristan blinked. "Excuse me?"

Hardaway walked over and grabbed him between his legs and squeezed his thigh.

His eyes widening, Tristan gasped, partly from shock and partly from pain. "Are you mad?"

"As I thought," Hardaway said. "You shouldn't be standing. You should rest."

"You done groping me?"

Hardaway removed his hand. "Groping you? I thought I was hired to help you recover from a grade three groin injury. Go inside and sit down. You shouldn't be standing if a simple touch is still painful."

Tristan crossed his arms over his chest. "I'm fine here, thanks."

"That wasn't a request," Hardaway said.

Heat rushed to Tristan's cheeks. No one ordered him around. No one.

Behind him, Lydia snickered—*little traitor*—and quickly started coughing.

"You're fired," Tristan gritted out.

"Tristan, I'm sorry—" Lydia started.

"Not you," Tristan said and looked at Hardaway. "You."

Hardaway didn't look concerned. If anything, something like amusement flickered in his eyes. "You can't fire me for doing my job. Actually, you can't fire me, full stop. You aren't the one who hired me: the football club you play for did. Now, go inside, Mr. DuVal." Hardaway's lips curled slightly.

God, Tristan wanted to wipe that smirk off his face. He glowered at the guy, but before he could say anything, Hardaway turned to Lydia.

"Zach Hardaway," he said with a nice smile, shaking Lydia's hand.

"L-lydia Esmond," she said softly, licking her lips. Was she actually batting her eyelashes at the guy?

"Stop drooling and put your tongue back in your mouth," Tristan told her. "It's disgusting."

Lydia flushed to the roots of her hair and glared at him.

Tristan just lifted his eyebrows and smiled.

"Are you always such a mean, tactless brat?" Hardaway said.

Tristan widened his eyes and gave him his best innocent look. "Me? I think you're confused."

"Yes, I'm confused," Hardaway said, studying Tristan. "You have the reputation of a nice, down-to-earth guy. I'm still wondering where he is."

Tristan smiled. "You've heard of me? Wait, are you a fan?"

Hardaway's lips twisted. "Hardly. I support Arsenal."

It figured. Loser.

As if he could read his thoughts, Hardaway let out a laugh. "Even if I liked your team, I wouldn't be your fan. I think your brother is the better player and should be the one playing on the left wing for Chelsea."

Paling with fury, Tristan balled his hands into fists. In his peripheral vision, he could see Lydia cringing at Hardaway's remark. She knew it was a very bad idea to even imply that his adoptive brother was a better player than him—because Gabriel *wasn't* the better player, dammit.

Screw good first impressions. That prick didn't deserve any niceties wasted on him.

"Oh yeah?" Tristan said, stepping closer to Hardaway. Their faces were inches away now. Up close, Hardaway's gaze was kind of unsettling. Not that Tristan let it show. And it was annoying that the guy was half a head taller than him—and Tristan was of perfectly normal height, thank you very much.

He locked his eyes with Hardaway's and said softly, "It takes very little to ruin one's career, you know. A few words to the wrong people would do the trick. If I were you, I'd be a little more respectful. I'm surprised you aren't starving on the streets if that's your usual attitude toward your clients. Be careful." He smiled sweetly. "Just a piece of friendly advice."

Hardaway's eyes narrowed, all traces of amusement disappearing from them. "It would take a lot more to ruin my career than some spoiled rich boy's words."

"Really?" Tristan said, cocking his head. "So sure of yourself?"

"I think you're misunderstanding something," Hardaway said slowly. "I don't need this job. My services are normally booked months in advance. I agreed to do this only as a favor to Jared Sheldon. So it's not me who should be careful, brat. If you don't like that I don't suck up to you like everyone else does—"

"How do you even know that?" Tristan said, curious despite himself. "That people 'suck up' to me?"

A smile appeared on Hardaway's lips.

"I've heard of you. I've been warned about you."

"By whom?" Tristan asked, but a suspicion was already forming in his mind. Now the guy's attitude was starting to make a lot more sense. "Not by my brother, by any chance?"

"Yes. By Gabriel."

Tristan laughed.

"Care to share the joke?" Hardaway said when Tristan's laughter died down.

"My so-called brother just hates that people like me more." Tristan lifted his hand and petted the guy's clean-shaven cheek. "You poor, naive thing. Gabe's just jealous of me, has always been. I'm more talented, good-looking, and intelligent."

"And more humble," Hardaway said.

"Humility is overrated," Tristan said with a smile, looking at him from under his eyelashes.

Hardaway's face remained impassive. He caught Tristan's wrist and pushed his hand away. "You can cut it out. Your baby blues don't work on me."

Tristan blinked, only now realizing what he'd been doing—attempting to do. He was so used to trying to make every person eat out of his hand that he barely noticed when he did it.

"Habit," he said with a scowl, averting his gaze. "And are you color blind? My eyes aren't baby blue. They're more green than blue."

"They're weird blue," Hardaway said, making Tristan's scowl deepen. He glanced at Tristan's groin. "I told you to go inside and sit down."

"And I told you I'm fine here," Tristan said. He wasn't being entirely truthful. His groin muscles were sore, and his discomfort was growing every time he shifted even a little, but he'd be damned if he admitted it and proved this insufferable prick right.

"If you say so," Hardaway said, shrugging. Nodding to Lydia, who was watching them curiously, Hardaway stalked away.

Tristan frowned. "Where are you going?"

"Home," Hardaway threw over his shoulder.

Tristan strode after him. "What? What about my injury? You can't leave without doing your job!"

"I'll come back when you stop being a baby and actually let me do my job. I work with adults."

"I didn't say you could go," Tristan hissed out, anger quickening his strides. What a presumptuous son of a bitch. "If I don't let you order me around, it doesn't mean you can just ditch the job you're paid for—Ow!" Tristan grabbed his upper thigh and came to a halt, swearing elaborately as a sharp, agonizing pain shot through his leg. He fell to one knee, cursing.

Hardaway was by his side immediately. "I fucking told you. You should be resting a groin injury, not putting it under unnecessary stress."

"Shut up," Tristan said, hissing as he tried to get onto his feet. Tried and failed. He made another attempt to stand up and whimpered.

Hardaway sighed. "For fuck's sake," he said before leaning down and scooping him into his arms. He threw Tristan over his shoulder like a sack of potatoes and headed toward the house.

"Put me down," Tristan said, flushing with humiliation. "I can walk."

Hardaway just snorted at that.

"Lead the way," he told Lydia. "His bedroom."

"This way," she said, walking ahead. At least she wasn't snickering at his expense again.

By the time they reached the bedroom, Tristan's lip was bloody; he had been biting it to keep himself from making any noise. God, it hurt.

He was relieved and a little surprised when Hardaway gently eased him onto the bed: he had expected him to be rough.

When Hardaway reached for the waistband of Tristan's sweatpants, Tristan grabbed his hand. "What are you doing?"

The guy gave him a weird look. "My job. I need to examine your groin."

Feeling silly, Tristan nodded reluctantly and told Lydia, "Out."

"Bring me an ice pack, a wet towel, and bandages," Hardaway told her.

She nodded and hurried out of the room.

Tristan looked at the ceiling while Hardaway pulled his sweatpants off, leaving him only in his briefs. Strong fingers touched his thighs, then his lower stomach and groin. Tristan grimaced. It didn't exactly feel pleasant. "Well?"

"It's been about ten days since you got injured, right?" Hardaway said.

"Yeah."

"The pain should have subsided by now," Hardaway said, sounding a little annoyed. "My presence here is pretty much pointless if we can't start doing massages and exercises, and we can't do it during the initial acute phase. It should have been over by now. Did you follow Jared's instructions?"

Tristan shrugged. "More or less."

"More or less?" Hardaway repeated.

"I'm not the type to sit still and twiddle my thumbs all day," Tristan said, still looking at the ceiling.

Hardaway took a deep breath and breathed out audibly.

Tristan suppressed a smile. Driving people crazy was one of his favorite things in the world.

"Look at me when I'm talking to you," Hardaway said.

Tristan met his eyes. "What?" he said, weirdly conscious of Hardaway's hands on his thighs.

"Jared told me you wanted to return to the pitch as soon as possible," Hardaway said. "Thanks to your own recklessness and stubbornness, you made your injury worse. You can't start training until the pain is mostly gone. You can only blame yourself if you miss the World Cup."

Tristan's lips thinned.

Lydia returned to the room and handed Hardaway what he had requested before leaving again. Silently, Hardaway sat down beside him, wrapped the ice pack in a wet towel, and pressed it firmly against Tristan's groin. "Do you now understand how stupid you've been?"

"I really don't like your attitude," Tristan replied.

Hardaway smiled. He was one of those people whose face didn't soften much with a smile. "Get used to it. I don't handle my patients with kid gloves."

Tristan only glowered at him.

For a few long minutes, there was only silence as they regarded each other. It was making Tristan feel a bit funny, but he refused to look away first.

Minutes later, Hardaway was the one who eventually did. He removed the ice pack and started wrapping the elastic bandage around his thigh. Passing the bandage around the back of Tristan's waist, he secured it.

"Now you must rest," Hardaway said, removing his hands. "And when I say rest, I mean it. Also, ice three times a day for fifteen minutes."

Tristan said nothing.

"Understood?" Hardaway said, in a tone that brooked no argument.

"I can't lounge in bed all day," Tristan said, trying to sound reasonable and adult. It grated on his nerves that Hardaway treated him as if he were a half-wit baby. "My muscles are getting weaker with every day. How am I supposed to regain fitness if I'm a couch potato?"

"We'll rebuild your muscles after the acute phase is over."

Tristan shook his head. "Do you have any idea how long I worked for this body?" He might have never been as scrawny and short as his brother, but he was naturally very lean and it had taken a lot of hard work to gain and maintain the muscle mass he had. And even with all the daily workouts, he would never be as well-muscled and strong as most footballers were. At least he was strong enough to not get bullied off the ball, as Gabriel often was.

Hardaway's gaze swept over Tristan's body.

Tristan fidgeted a little. It was silly. He had nothing to be ashamed of—although he was just of medium height, he had a great body—but this guy's scrutiny made him feel oddly self-conscious, and he hated feeling self-conscious. He was Tristan DuVal. He was rich, handsome, and popular. His days of being a thin, unwashed kid were long over.

When Hardaway returned his gaze to Tristan's face, his eyes were unreadable. "It's nothing we can't fix."

Tristan pursed his lips. "Fine. But I'll want a full body massage. I can feel my muscles getting weak and stiff."

Hardaway gave him a pinched look. "All right," he said after a moment of consideration, opening the bag that had been slung over his shoulder. He pulled out a bottle of massage oil. "Lose the shirt and turn on your stomach."

Tristan pulled his shirt off, rolled onto his belly, and closed his eyes.

He caught his lip between his teeth, suddenly acutely aware that he was wearing his briefs and nothing else. His own unease puzzled him a little. He was used to getting massages from the club's physiotherapists—heck, he was used to being completely naked during those massages. In fact, the only reason Hardaway hadn't told him to lose the briefs too was probably because Tristan's groin couldn't be massaged while his injury was still inflamed.

"What are you waiting for? I'm getting cold," Tristan said, his irritation growing along with his self-consciousness. This man made him feel too uneasy and on edge, for no discernible reason.

He heard Hardaway open the bottle.

And then—

"You're supposed to warm it up, you idiot!"

"It's the second time you called me an idiot. I'm getting offended." Hardaway put his oiled hands on the base of Tristan's neck and—

"Ow! That hurts!"

"Don't be a little girl."

"But it hurts."

"Come on, it's not that bad."

"You aren't the one being—ow!"

Hardaway chuckled, digging his fingers harder. "Baby."

"I don't think I know you well enough to let you use endearments," Tristan said, his voice silky-soft.

"I told you to cut it out," Hardaway said dryly. "Your ridiculous bedroom voice is wasted on me."

Grinning, Tristan said in a low, intimate voice, "Does my teasing make you uncomfortable, Zachary?"

Hardaway snorted, his big hands stroking and kneading along Tristan's spine. "My name is Zach. Only my mother calls me Zachary."

"You didn't answer the question."

Zach made an irritated sound. "No, it doesn't make me uncomfortable. I just don't like games. I don't like bullshit."

"And what do you like?"

"I prefer honesty and straight-forwardness."

"Boring," Tristan said, scrunching his nose. "Then what do you do for fun?"

"Watch football. Fuck," Zach said in a conversational tone.

Tristan laughed. "Wait, let me guess: you've been fucking the same person for years."

"I've had one girlfriend for years—"

"See!"

"I'll have to disappoint you," Zach said, pressing his thumbs into Tristan's lower back, hard. "We're in an open relationship."

"How progressive of you," Tristan said, though he was genuinely surprised. The guy didn't strike him as the type to be in an open relationship. "Why? How does it even work?"

"Not that it's any of your business, but when two people trust each other, it's only practical. She's a sports journalist. We're both away a lot and often don't see each other for months."

Zach continued massaging his lower back. It felt...it didn't suck.

"Hmm, so you're both free to sleep with anyone you want?"

"Yes."

"And you never feel grossed out that another man touched your girlfriend?"

The concept was a little hard to grasp for Tristan, but then again, he'd never been all that good at sharing his things.

"I'm not the jealous type," Zach said. "We're both adults, and we both have physical needs. It's only practical."

"And she doesn't get jealous either?" That, Tristan had trouble believing, considering...well, he wasn't blind. Zach was a dick, but he was a hot dick.

"She knows sex doesn't mean much if there is no real emotional attachment. She knows she's the only one who matters."

Tristan kind of wanted to meet the woman now. She must be very sure of herself...or very foolish.

"Anyway," Zach said, still kneading his lower back. "It won't matter soon. We've agreed we'll be exclusive after the wedding."

Tristan opened his eyes. "You're getting married? When?"

"In three months."

"My sincere condolences."

Zach gave a chuckle as he moved to massage Tristan's legs, skipping his buttocks and thighs. "Are you a commitment-phobe?"

"I just don't see the point. Long-term relationships are restrictive and boring."

The hands shifted to his calves, kneading them hard. "Have you ever been in a relationship, little boy?" Zach's voice practically dripped with condescension.

Tristan kicked him—and then promptly groaned as a jolt of pain shot through his groin.

"If you keep this up, you won't recover any time soon," Zach said.

"Says the guy who provoked me," Tristan grumbled, suppressing the urge to turn his head and stick his tongue out. God, what was it about this guy that brought out the worst in him? He couldn't remember the last time he felt so on edge and childish.

"Turn onto your back," Zach said.

Grunting, Tristan did, and Hardaway started massaging his front.

Tristan squirmed a little. He was so used to getting massages that he'd stopped finding them strange and intrusive a long time ago, but for some reason…this time it was different. Zach's touch was impersonal, his hands gliding over Tristan's skin with practiced efficiency, but Tristan couldn't look away from Zach's hands as they kneaded and stroked the muscles of his arm.

He felt eyes on his face and looked up. Zach was watching him.

As soon as their eyes met, Zach looked away, focusing

on the task at hand.

It made Tristan wonder. "What?"

"Nothing," Zach said gruffly, moving to sit just above Tristan's head. He placed the heels of his hands just below Tristan's clavicle. Then he pushed his hands down, palming the pectorals and kneading them.

Tristan watched Zach's hands glide over his chest, covering his nipples, the palms rubbing against them, again and again. Tristan bit the inside of his cheek, feeling a stirring in his groin. Fuck. This hadn't happened to him in ages during a massage. He knew it was a pretty normal reaction, and most physios weren't bothered by it when it happened, but the fact that it was happening with this prick was mortifying. He closed his eyes, thinking of the most disgusting things he could.

"You'll need a new bed," Zach said.

Tristan's eyes flew open.

"What? Why?"

"The mattress is far too soft."

Tristan ground his teeth. Unbelievable. "No one asked your opinion on my *mattress*. I'll have you know, I'm very fond of my mattress."

Zach's hands—finally—stopped stroking his chest. He moved down, to work on Tristan's legs. "It's bad for your spine."

"My mattress is perfect."

"No, it isn't," Zach said. "It needs to support your body in a neutral position, in which your spine has a nice curvature and your buttocks, shoulders, and head are supported in proper alignment. It's necessary for your bones to have some resistance. Your mattress is too soft for that."

"But if the mattress is firm, it will push on those pressure points," Tristan said.

"Yes, but only if the mattress is too firm. If it's too soft, like your mattress, those pressure points won't be properly supported, so your whole body flops back." Zach pushed him onto his side. "See," Zach said, laying a hand on his nape. He slowly dragged the hand down Tristan's spine to his lower back, just above his ass. "Your spine is curved because the mattress sinks under your weight too much. It can cause various issues in the long run. It can worsen…"

Zach was still saying something—lecturing him—but Tristan had trouble focusing.

Zach's hand was resting just above his ass.

"…Do you now understand why you need a new mattress?"

"All right, whatever!" Tristan grumbled, squirming away from Zach's hand. "All you ever do is criticize me."

"Ever?" Zach said, his gray eyes flashing with humor. "We met half an hour ago."

"Precisely. I've heard more criticism in half an hour than I've heard in half a year."

"That means you're just surrounded by suck-ups." Zach stood up, wiping his hands with a towel. "I'll choose a new mattress for you. You will be a good boy and sleep on the mattress I order for you."

For some stupid reason, Tristan's cock twitched. He tried to ignore it. "You're crossing the line," Tristan said, very, very softly.

Zach smiled. "I don't think so. It's the job of the physiotherapist to make sure his patient is in top form. And you'll find that I take my job very seriously."

He grabbed his bag and headed to the door.

"Any other orders?" Tristan said at his back.

"Don't do anything stupid just to spite me," Zach said over his shoulder. "I'll return tomorrow morning and I expect to find you still in bed."

"Am I allowed to get up to pee, my lord?"

"Only if you really have to," Zach said. "I can tell Lydia to buy diapers for you. Baby."

Tristan grabbed a pillow and threw it at the prick's head.

Zach ducked, laughing.

Chapter 2

Zach Hardaway was a tyrant.

At least that was what Tristan was convinced of as he stared at the unappetizing mess on his plate.

"I'm not gonna eat this," he said. "Give me back my hot dog." To be honest, he didn't want it all that much; it was the principle of the thing.

"No," Zach said. "You eat too much unhealthy food."

"I happen to like my unhealthy food. One hot dog won't kill me."

"One hot dog won't, but Lydia told me all you eat is fast food and sweets."

Tristan raised his chin a notch. "So what? I'm young. I have a fast metabolism, I train every day—I used to—"

"You'll thank me when you're older," Zach said. "A regular fare of hot dogs can do more than raise your cholesterol and blood pressure levels. Processed meat can increase the risk for diabetes, heart disease, and a few types of cancer. Actually, eating a hot dog every day can increase your risk of colorectal cancer by twenty—"

"I feel so sorry for your fiancée. Poor woman. To marry such a bore."

"Odd," Zach said, his eyes gleaming with amusement. "Donna just told me a week ago that she was the luckiest woman in the world."

"She's delusional," Tristan grumbled, stabbing the mess on his plate with his fork. "And I hate you."

"I'm not here to become your best friend," Zach said. "Now eat."

Tristan scowled darkly—and ate.

* * *

Three days later, Tristan stormed into his doctor's office and demanded,

"I want you to fire him."

Dr. Jared Sheldon lifted his eyes from his computer.

Despite his annoyance, as always, Tristan couldn't help but stare a little. With his dark blue eyes, dark hair and perfect bone structure, Jared Sheldon was easily the most handsome man he'd ever seen. But handsome or not, it was all Jared's fault. Jared was the one who had hired *him*.

"What are you doing here?" Jared said. "Does walking still hurt?"

"Yes, but—"

"Then you're supposed to be resting," Jared said. "The general rule of thumb is if an activity brings any pain or discomfort, stop doing it immediately."

"That's what he said, too," Tristan muttered. "I want you to get rid of him."

Leaning back, Jared gave him a patient look. "I presume you're talking about your new physiotherapist?"

"Who else? I want you to fire him."

"Why?"

Tristan shoved his hands into his pockets, dropping his eyes for a moment. He had to actually bite his tongue to prevent himself from calling Zach names. Contrary to what Zach thought, he *wasn't* a baby. God, he hated how childish and impulsive Zach made him feel. "I don't like him."

"I'm afraid that's not a good enough reason," Jared said. "You know how understaffed we are—"

"I'm the star of this team." Tristan smiled at him. "It's in your best interests to get me back to fitness as soon as possible. Isn't that your job, Jared?"

Jared narrowed his eyes. "I'm well aware of what my job is. I'm responsible for rehabilitation of all footballers of this club, and no one is entitled to preferential treatment. Because of the onslaught of injuries in the first team, reserve team and under-18 team, our physios are overworked already."

"But—"

"Tristan," Jared cut him off, leveling him with a look. "I asked Zach Hardaway to work with you as a personal favor to me. He's one of the best physiotherapists and fitness trainers in Europe. You're incredibly lucky he agreed to do it on such short notice. Normally it would be impossible. He's in very high demand."

Tristan scoffed. "That explains why he's such a bossy asshole."

Jared pinched the bridge of his nose.

"If you want to return to the pitch before the end of the season and get called up for the English National Team, you will do what he says. And no, you can't hire another physiotherapist—I won't clear you if Zach doesn't confirm you're fully recovered and fit to play. After all the trouble I went through to get you the best physiotherapist, you won't get him fired only because you don't like him." Jared's voice softened. "It's for your own good, Tristan."

Tristan clenched his jaw. In other words, Jared was telling him to suck it up and deal with it. But Jared was mistaken if he thought Tristan would let Jared paint him into a corner. He never let anyone do it. He hadn't let people do it even when he had been a kid.

Tristan considered his options. He hadn't wanted to do this, but desperate times called for desperate measures.

He said softly, "If you don't fire him, someone might accidentally find out that you're fucking my brother. That would be such a shame. His career would be ruined."

Jared went very still, his knuckles going white as he gripped the pen he was holding.

Tristan felt a pang of regret. He liked Jared. He did. Jared had always been kind to him, despite Gabe's attempts to convince him what a piece of shit Tristan was.

And he had just proved Gabe right.

The feeling of regret grew heavier as Tristan watched Jared's eyes harden. Had he made a mistake?

"Nice," a familiar voice said from behind him. "Blackmail, brat?"

Pursing his lips, Tristan turned his head and glowered at Zach.

Zach stepped into the room, his steely gray eyes fixing Tristan with a hard look. "Why aren't you in bed? I gave you clear instructions."

Tristan scowled. "You mean orders?"

"Precisely," Zach said, undeterred. "I need to talk to Jared. Go wait for me outside."

The nerve of him.

Tristan gave him a mutinous glare. Zach just looked at him expectantly. The infuriating part was that there was something about this man that made Tristan *want* to obey him. And it pissed him off.

Tristan stormed out of the room—well, attempted to—but pain shot through his groin and he couldn't hold back a whimper. Grabbing his groin, Tristan slowed down.

"Shut up," he threw over his shoulder.

"I didn't say anything," Zach said wryly. "But if you stop being a baby and start listening to me, you'll recover twice as fast."

"I hate you," Tristan said with feeling and slammed the door behind him.

Outside Jared's office, he flopped down on the couch, angry and more than a little puzzled. God, what was wrong with him? Tristan DuVal didn't obey anyone. Tristan DuVal didn't let anyone order him around. He was the one who cajoled and manipulated people. He had everyone eating out of his hand. Why did he let that high-handed asshole dictate what he did? Zach had told him to wait outside and he had *obeyed*, like a good little boy. Unbelievable.

He didn't understand his own behavior and it bothered him. Tristan would be the first to admit his moral compass was probably pretty skewed by most people's standards, and he saw nothing wrong with telling people a white lie to get what he wanted, but he always prided himself on being brutally honest with himself. He knew his mind and he wasn't prone to self-delusion.

But this time he had no clue what was going on. He didn't recognize himself. He was behaving like a…like a foolish boy. Since the moment he'd met Zach Hardaway, he'd been making mistake after mistake. The smart thing to do would have been to be nice to Zach from the very beginning. One could catch more flies with honey than vinegar: that was practically Tristan's motto. But when it came to Zach, his temper always got the better of him and he spoke before he thought. It was downright stupid and shortsighted, and Tristan was never stupid and shortsighted—well, normally.

The sound of footsteps interrupted his musings and Tristan lifted his head. He suppressed a sigh upon seeing Gabriel, his adoptive brother and a constant thorn in his side.

"What are you doing here?" Gabriel said suspiciously, glancing at the door to Jared's office.

"Just finished having wild sex with Dr. Sheldon."

"You're so full of shit," Gabe said with an eye-roll before disappearing into the office of his…lover? Boyfriend? Best friend? Gabe's relationship with Jared had always confused Tristan. It had always been so weird and freakishly close that it bordered on codependent and unhealthy. It was almost a relief to know that they were fucking now—it was easier to put a label on their relationship.

Tristan didn't really understand what Jared saw in his brother, but he wasn't blind. It was a wonder they hadn't been outed yet, so nauseatingly besotted with each other they looked whenever Tristan had seen them together.

Tristan shook his head. Gabe was an idiot to risk his career, no matter how handsome Jared Sheldon was. They were professional footballers. They were constantly in the spotlight. The risk of being outed was enormous. That was why Tristan was so careful when he got laid. Having an actual relationship with a man was incredibly risky for a football player. Well, it was Gabe's problem, not his. If the little idiot wanted to risk his career for a dick, it was his own choice.

Tristan looked at the door to Jared's office again.

All right, enough was enough.

He got to his feet, opened the door, and stuck his head in.

Zach was chatting amiably with Jared and Gabe.

"Seriously?" Tristan said. "You're making me wait so you can make small talk? I'm leaving."

"I'm done," Zach said. "We can go now."

Tristan's eyes flicked to the wedding invitations on the desk.

"You could have mailed them," he said before striding away.

"Slow down, brat," Zach called after him. "I'm not carrying you again if you worsen your injury—again."

Tristan ignored him, his mood souring further for no discernible reason.

It didn't take Zach long to catch up to him. He grabbed Tristan's arm, forcing him to slow down. "Come to complain about me, huh?"

"Yes," Tristan bit out before smiling cheerfully and waving to the people they encountered. "Hey!"

Zach chuckled. "You're such a chameleon."

"Thanks," Tristan said.

"That wasn't a compliment."

Tristan turned his head and smiled. "I know."

For a moment, Zach's eyes lingered on him before Zach looked away.

As they left the building, a cold March wind whistled through the air, biting Tristan's face.

"Zip up your jacket," Zach said.

Tristan zipped up his jacket. He wasn't obeying Zach. It was just really cold. "Are you this charming with all your patients, or am I just lucky?" he said.

A faint smile twisted Zach's lips. "With all my patients, but you bring out the worst in me."

Oddly, that pleased Tristan.

"Did you drive here?" Zach said. When Tristan shook his head, he said, "Good. I'll drive you back to your place." He opened the door of his car and got in the driver's seat.

"So what are we doing today?" Tristan said, getting into the passenger's seat. "Nothing again? Do I get another lecture?"

"Actually, we might finally start the rehabilitation program if the swelling is completely gone. It looked better yesterday."

"About time," Tristan muttered.

They drove in silence for a while.

"Tell me about your girlfriend," Tristan said at last, bored of silence.

"Why?"

Tristan glanced at him. "Why not?"

"I've already told you more than I should have. I normally like to keep my personal life apart from my professional one. Mixing them is never a good idea."

"You should tell that to your friend."

Zach frowned. "You mean Jared?"

"Do you know another doctor shagging his patient?"

Zach let out a low chuckle. "If you mean Gabriel, they're just friends. Very close friends, but that's it. I know it's an easy mistake to make—I thought they were an item too when I met them a couple of years ago. But they're just friends."

"Oh yeah," Tristan said, not without sarcasm. "Last week, I saw Gabe sucking Jared's dick in his car. It looked real friendly."

That silenced Zach.

At last, he said, "So it's not just some bullshit you made up to force Jared to fire me."

"Nope." Tristan flickered his eyes to Zach. His face was hard to read. "So, what do you think of it?"

"It's none of my business. It's none of your business, either."

Tristan gave a non-committal shrug.

"Tristan."

"What?"

"It's none of your business. And don't even think about blackmailing Jared again."

Tristan sighed. "You're no fun. Fine." He added quickly, "I'm not *obeying* you. I just realize it wasn't the smartest thing to do."

"It wasn't," Zach said.

"What about you?" Tristan asked after a while. "Ever fucked a patient?"

Zach didn't say anything, his gaze firmly on the road ahead.

His eyes widening, Tristan grinned. "You have! You so have! Ha! You aren't so perfect after all."

"It was years ago," Zach said curtly. "I was young and inexperienced and she needed comfort. I didn't know how to draw the line—a common mistake many physios make. I never repeated the same mistake again."

"Wait, is that why you're so dictatorial and insensitive with your patients now? Because you want them to hate you?"

"I'm not insensitive," Zach said.

"At least you don't deny the dictatorial part."

The corner of Zach's mouth curled up. "Habit. I have five younger siblings."

"Poor things," Tristan murmured. "So what happened to the woman?"

"What woman?"

"The one you slept with. Your patient."

"None of your business."

"Oh, come on!"

"We both agreed it was a mistake," Zach said. "And it was. It was a long time ago. I barely remember her."

Tristan studied him with interest.

"Tell me about your girlfriend, then."

"No. I already told you that."

"But why not?"

"Because it's none of your business."

Tristan exhaled loudly. The worst part was, he knew Zach was riling him up on purpose. Tristan knew it because he did the same thing with Lydia just for the fun of it. Zach's face was stern, but there was definitely a hint of amusement lurking in his eyes.

"You're so enjoying this," Tristan said.

"Yep. You're amusing when you pout. Such a diva."

"I don't pout."

"Sure."

Tristan crossed his arms over his chest and said nothing.

When Zach finally parked the car in front of Tristan's house, they looked at each other.

"Still pouting?" Zach said.

Tristan nodded with a serene smile.

Chuckling, Zach shook his head. "I've seen some post-match interviews with you before. You're so different from your public persona."

Tristan rolled his eyes. "I know I'm not gonna like it, but let's hear it."

Zach's lips twitched. "In every interview you're always so charming, easy-going, and smiley. You're likable. So damn likable that my bullshit radar went off every time I saw you say all the right things and wrap people around your little finger."

"It's called charisma," Tristan said haughtily.

Zach snorted a laugh. "I don't think so. People are just fooled by your pretty face and a pair of pretty blue eyes."

Tristan batted his eyelashes. "Aw, you think I'm pretty?"

He received a flat look from Zach. "As a physiotherapist and personal trainer, I've learned a long time ago to look at a human body objectively. And objectively, you're the prettiest guy I've ever seen."

Tristan smiled. Of course he knew he looked good; he didn't suffer from false modesty.

Tristan glanced at the mirror. Messy brown hair, high cheekbones, flawless warm-colored skin, full lips and blue-green eyes. Yep, he'd totally hit that.

"There's Jared, though," Tristan said. "He's totally the

most handsome man I've ever seen."

Zach shot him a sharp look before scoffing and getting out of the car. "I said pretty, not handsome."

"I sense a not-so-subtle insult to my masculinity," Tristan said, getting out and closing the door.

Zach was already walking toward the house. "Come on, let's have a look at your groin and see if the swelling is gone."

A little puzzled by the sudden change of topic, Tristan followed him.

Five minutes later, Tristan found himself in his gym downstairs, sitting on the couch as Zach knelt in front of him and examined his thigh.

It was quiet in the house. Tristan looked at his jeans on the floor. "See, the swelling is gone," he said. "I told you I was fine to start training." The swelling really was gone, and the bruising had faded considerably, too. His injury didn't trouble him as much as it used to—only when he moved too abruptly.

Zach carefully prodded his flesh. He stroked Tristan's thigh, applying some pressure. "Does it hurt when I do this?"

"Not really."

The fingers moved to Tristan's upper thigh and pressed. "Now?"

Tristan shook his head.

"All right," Zach said. "I'm going to take your briefs off." He wasn't asking. He didn't need to ask. It was a completely normal thing to do for a physiotherapist.

Tristan watched as Zach laid his hands on his hips. They looked dark against his skin, and Tristan was by no means pale.

The hands tugged Tristan's briefs down his thighs. It was something many other physios had done in the past, and Zach's touch was no different: professional and impersonal.

But there was nothing professional or impersonal about the way Tristan's body reacted.

Zach's hands went still on his thighs, his eyes on Tristan's half-hard cock.

Tristan wondered if it was possible to die from mortification. He averted his gaze, feeling betrayed by his own stupid body. What was wrong with him?

"I haven't got laid in months," he said.

Zach remained silent. His hands resumed moving and quickly removed Tristan's briefs.

"The skin of my thighs is just very sensitive," Tristan said.

"You don't have to be so defensive."

Tristan barely stopped himself from kicking him. He refrained from doing so only because of his injury: he wouldn't give Zach another reason to scold him in his oh-so-superior tone. Not that Zach needed a reason.

"I'm not being defensive," Tristan said. He was pretty proud of how even and calm his voice sounded.

"Of course not," Zach said, moving his hand up, his fingers less than an inch from Tristan's cock. He stroked his groin. "Does this hurt?" Before Tristan could shake his head, Zach pressed his finger hard into the muscle.

Tristan sucked a breath in. "Yeah." Thankfully, the pain dealt with his little problem. He was almost soft again. Almost. "You're fit enough to start a gradual rehabilitation program," Zach said, to Tristan's surprise. "Stretching and strengthening exercises."

"We'll start with gentle static stretches. Remember that stretching exercises should be pain free. If it hurts, you'll stop. We'll move to more dynamic exercises when you're ready. Same with strengthening exercises—we'll increase the load through the muscles gradually."

"When?"

The gray eyes looked at him steadily. "The key word is gradually."

"But—"

"It's not up for a debate. Yes, Jared told me you wanted to return as soon as possible, but you'll be back when you're ready, and not a minute sooner." Zach smiled a little. "And quit giving me that look. You look ridiculous."

"What look?"

"The puppy-dog-eyes look. It doesn't work on me. I have five younger siblings. I'm immune to that shit."

"I'm not giving you puppy-dog-eyes," Tristan said distractedly, acutely aware of Zach's hands on his thighs. They were so big. It was a bit of a weakness of his. He liked men with strong and capable hands. And this prick's hands were perfect. They made him think of sex.

"Is it really necessary for you to keep your hands on my thighs?" Tristan said, a little sharper than he had intended.

Zach looked down, as if only now realizing where his hands were. Tristan had hoped to make him uncomfortable, but Zach didn't look flustered at all. "I don't know," he said, his gaze shifting to Tristan's cock— which was half-hard again. "You seem to like it a great deal."

Tristan's face grew warm.

"You smug, conceited— I told you my thighs were very sensitive."

"Too bad for you, then," Zach said. "Now that the swelling is gone, I'm going to massage them every day, especially after your exercises. Speaking of exercises..."

Zach pulled Tristan's briefs up and got to his feet. "We'll start with very gentle stretching. Short adductor stretch, long adductor stretch and hip flexors."

Nodding, Tristan slipped into his gym shorts and sat down on the mat.

"Bend your knees," Zach instructed. "Now gently press down with the elbows onto the knees to increase the stretch—"

"I know how to do it," Tristan said as he felt a gentle stretching in the inner thigh. Although it wasn't really painful, it felt a little uncomfortable.

"Hold for half a minute," Zach said, ignoring his words. As if Tristan hadn't said anything.

Tristan glared up at him.

"Now a long adductor stretch," Zach said, a corner of his mouth twitching up. He crossed his arms over his chest. "Since you know how to do everything. Obviously you don't need my help."

Tristan hesitated. He wasn't sure which stretch it was, but he'd be damned if he admitted it now.

He stood up and put his feet apart. Looking at Zach and trying to gauge if he was doing the right stretch, he bent the left knee out to the side and leaned to the left.

"Good," Zach said and Tristan smiled in triumph— until Zach spoke again. "But that's not the stretch I meant."

Tristan scowled. "I'm pretty sure this one stretches the long adductor muscle."

"It does," Zach said. "But I wanted you to do something else."

"Too bad for you, then," Tristan said in a mocking voice, throwing Zach's own words back at him. "I'm done stretching the long adductor muscle."

A muscle twitched in Zach's lean cheek. "Sit on the mat."

Tristan didn't move.

"Sit."

Tristan didn't move.

Zach took a step toward him and another, his brows drawn together and his jaw working. "Do you enjoy being difficult?"

"Yep," Tristan murmured, looking him in the eye. "But clearly not as much as you enjoy bossing me around."

They glared at each other from a few inches apart.

The silence stretched.

Tristan's heart beat so fast, he could almost feel the adrenaline rushing through his veins. "I did stretch the long adductor muscle. I don't have to do anything else only because you get a kick out of watching me do as you say."

Zach's hand twitched toward him before Zach clasped both hands behind his back. "I am your physiotherapist," he said, his calm tone at odds with the intensity in his eyes. "You will do as I say if you want to get fit. It's as simple as that."

"You're my physiotherapist, not my boss."

"When it concerns your recovery, I'm your boss."

Tristan raised his brows. "And what are you gonna do if I refuse to do as you say? Spank me?"

A strange expression crossed Zach's face. "You think I wouldn't?"

Tristan smiled. "I dare you to try!"

Zach's nostrils flared. "Don't tempt me." He stepped back. "On the mat," he barked out.

Tristan's retort died in his throat. Zach was truly angry now—far angrier than the situation called for. Why?

Slowly, Tristan sat down, eyeing his physio curiously.

"Legs as far apart as possible and knees straight," Zach said, his tone still harsh. "Keep your back straight and lean forward."

Tristan did as he was told.

"Hold for twenty seconds."

The seconds ticked by.

"Hip flexors," Zach said, sounding a little calmer now.

Tristan did the required stretches without any comment.

When he was done, Zach turned away. "You will do all of them four times a day. Five, if you don't feel sore."

And then he was gone, leaving Tristan staring after him, frustrated and a great deal puzzled.

Chapter 3

The next day, Zach was back to his normal bossy and slightly aloof self, the wry curl to his lips firmly back. The brimming anger of the previous day was nowhere to be seen. It was a mystery. Tristan could never resist a mystery.

"I want a full-body massage," Tristan told him after he finished doing the exercises under Zach's supervision. "It's been days and I'm sore."

Zach nodded and retrieved the massage oil from his bag. "Undress and get on your belly."

Tristan pulled his t-shirt off and shimmied out of his shorts and briefs.

Naked, he got onto the massage table. It was new, just like the brand new bed upstairs. Just like the assortment of "healthy" food in his fridge. It was pretty disturbing how Zach had managed to change so many things in his life in such a short time.

Zach threw a towel over Tristan's hips. That surprised him a little. Unless asked, the team physiotherapists didn't bother preserving footballers' modesty—if such a thing even existed. It was difficult to care about modesty after long, brutal games, when their bodies ached and hurt.

Zach obviously knew that, as a professional sportsman, Tristan was used to massages, and that he didn't really need to cover Tristan to preserve his non-existent modesty.

Did his nudity bother Zach?

The thought intrigued him.

He was pretty sure Zach was straight—he was getting married, for fuck's sake—but...

But.

Tristan closed his eyes when Zach started massaging his neck.

As Zach's strong oiled fingers kneaded his stiff muscles, Tristan's thoughts went back to the towel covering his ass. "Do you think I'm attractive?"

The hands paused on his shoulder blades. "What kind of question is that?"

"A simple one," Tristan said, without opening his eyes.

"You know you're attractive," Zach said with some irritation in his voice. "And I answered the question yesterday."

"I'm not asking about your professional objective opinion. Do you find me attractive? What one finds attractive is subjective."

A long silence.

"I'm straight," Zach said, as if it was an answer. Before Tristan could tell him that it wasn't, Zach continued, a hint of a smile in his voice, "And I'm sure I wouldn't find you attractive if I were gay. Gay men probably don't like feminine guys."

"Feminine?" Tristan spluttered, outraged. "There's nothing feminine about me! Does this body look feminine to you?"

Zach actually had the nerve to laugh. "I'm talking about your face. You're too pretty for a man, dollface. Men aren't supposed to have eyes and lips like that."

"Oh yeah? You seem to have given it a lot of thought."

But once again, Zach didn't rise to the bait, and his voice was calm as he replied, "You have the sort of face that draws attention, and my job is to pay attention to the details. Your body is my job. I study it, I learn it, and then I improve it. Nothing more, nothing less."

Tristan pursed his lips.

Zach's hands moved to his lower back and started kneading there. Oh. Had he just gotten used to Zach's hands? They didn't seem that rough anymore. They felt...they felt good. Strong, capable, a little rough... just perfect.

Zach removed the towel and laid his hands on his buttocks. Tristan tensed and opened his eyes as Zach's hands started stroking and kneading his cheeks.

Tristan stared at the wall. It was just a massage. Just a massage. As usual, Zach's touch was absolutely impersonal and professional. It was no different than getting a massage from Ron or Gary, the team physiotherapists who usually rubbed him down after a long match.

It should have been no different.

Tristan's eyes closed again. He had to swallow back a moan. He hadn't lied yesterday: his skin really was extremely sensitive, especially down there, but it was usually easy to keep his arousal at bay when he was massaged. He was puzzled and annoyed that he didn't seem to be able to do it now.

Finally, Zach moved lower, but it helped very little. If anything, those big hands, stroking and kneading his thighs, only made his problem worse.

His cock was fully hard now, his body tingling all over, his nipples tight and aching. Tristan swallowed another moan, more than a little bewildered. He couldn't remember ever being so turned on by an impersonal sports massage.

There was a simple explanation, though. He'd gone too long without a nice, thick cock in him. He just needed to get laid—discreetly—and then he would stop reacting so ridiculously to a simple massage from a man he didn't even like.

"On your back," Zach said.

Explanation found and decision made, Tristan relaxed and rolled onto his back. He could still barely meet Zach's eyes when Zach saw his erection.

They stared at each other.

Zach snorted and started working on his shoulders. "It's a physiological response to touch. It happens all the time and it's nothing to be embarrassed of."

"I'm not embarrassed," Tristan said. Being embarrassed implied having something to be embarrassed of, which he most definitely didn't.

"Then why are you blushing?"

Great. He was blushing now? He never blushed.

"Just imagined having your cock in me."

Zach's eyes snapped to him, his hands going utterly still. It would have been comical if Tristan didn't feel like cutting his own tongue. Where the fuck had that come from?

The silence stretched.

Tristan smiled and forced out a laugh. "Ha ha! You have no sense of humor."

"And you have a very strange one," Zach said after a moment, returning to the task at hand.

He finished the massage quickly, ignoring Tristan's erection, and stepped away. "Tomorrow we might add a few more exercises," he said, washing his hands, his back to Tristan. "Maybe a very gentle static ball squeeze—"

"Can I have sex?"

Zach paused before turning around. "Absolutely not," he said, crossing his arms over his chest. "Sex is off-limits."

"You're so bloody predictable," Tristan grumbled, reaching for his clothes.

"If you want to recover as soon as possible, you must lay off sex."

"Tell that to my dick."

"You have a functional right hand," Zach said. "Have a wank."

Tristan threw the wet towel at his head.

Zach ducked. "It's a wonder you score any goals," he said, his lips twitching. "Your aim is incredibly poor."

Tristan grabbed the massage oil.

This time he didn't miss.

* * *

"You could have maimed me."

Tristan rolled his eyes, pressing the ice pack to Zach's right eye. "And you call me a drama queen."

Zach's left eye glared at him. He didn't look amused at all. "That bottle weighs half a pound, Tristan," he gritted out. "And you threw it at my face."

"It's not my fault your reflexes are incredibly poor," Tristan said with a sweet smile, pressing the ice harder to the rapidly swelling flesh.

He received another baleful look from the left eye. "I'm supposed to participate in a photo shoot for the wedding."

"Then you should thank me for saving you from it."

"And what am I supposed to tell her?"

"Who?"

"Donna."

"Donna?" Tristan said with feigned confusion.

"My fiancée," Zach said slowly. "The woman I'm marrying."

"Ah." Tristan moved closer in order to press the ice pack to Zach's cheekbone. It wasn't the most comfortable position. He was aware that his thigh was practically straddling Zach's. Too aware. "I guess you can tell her the truth. You can tell her what a dick you were and that you entirely deserved it."

"Is that what it looks like from your perspective?"

"Nope, that's just the truth." Tristan dropped himself on Zach lap, giving up all pretenses of not straddling him. When Zach raised his eyebrows, Tristan scowled. "If I have to play doctor for you, I'm not going to strain my own injury. I shouldn't even be doing this." He added with a cheeky smile, "You have a functional right hand, after all."

Zach let out a laugh. "And you have the memory of an elephant. You're doing this because it's your bloody fault."

"It's yours," Tristan said, sinking his fingers into Zach's thick hair and yanking hard, forcing him to turn his face a little. Zach said something scathing, and Tristan said something equally scathing back, but it all seemed distant, irrelevant, stupid. His heart was pounding, his skin felt too warm, Zach's thigh was hard under him, and he just couldn't concentrate. Couldn't think.

Goddammit.

Tristan always tried to be honest with himself. He knew what this was. Of course he knew. It didn't take a genius. Sitting so close to Zach—in his *lap*—was turning him into an idiot who wondered what Zach's cock looked like and whether it was as big and thick as those hands—and what it would feel like in his mouth.

God. If Zach hadn't been someone he strongly disliked, someone who infuriated him, frustrated him and made him feel inferior and *stupid,* Tristan wouldn't have been so angry with himself. He would have just gone for it, as he always did when he wanted something—or someone—badly enough. He knew he was attractive. He knew he was attractive enough to make even straight men bi-curious. But this was Zach fucking Hardaway. There was no way in hell Tristan was going to come on to him. He could easily imagine the superior, disgusted look on Zach's face if Zach realized that he wanted him—that Tristan was gagging for his cock. A wave of humiliation swept through him at the mere thought. How pathetic it would look.

Though, he didn't *want* Zach. His stupid body was just horny and seemed to like the idea of getting under his dick of a personal trainer.

He just needed to get laid and then all this silliness would go away.

"I'm done playing doctor," Tristan said curtly, dropping the ice pack and sliding off Zach's lap as casually as possible. Avoiding looking at Zach, he headed to the door. "Get out of my house. Why are you always in my house?"

Zach muttered something under his breath, too quietly for him to hear, before following him out of the gym.

Tristan didn't turn around, but he could feel Zach right behind him—could feel him with every inch of his body. Zach's eyes must be on the same level as Tristan's ass. Was Zach looking?

Tristan cringed, disgusted with his train of thought. Millions years of evolution and humans were still no better than animals.

Mindless animals driven by base instincts. He didn't like the guy one bit. Zach had quickly replaced his brother as the person Tristan couldn't stand the most.

But it didn't change the fact that a part of him wanted to turn around, shove Zach against the wall, and climb him like a tree.

Tristan set his jaw. He was going to get laid tonight, his injury be damned.

Chapter 4

The problem with being a famous footballer was that Tristan couldn't just go to a gay bar and pull someone when he wanted to get laid.

He couldn't screw some random stranger who might sell the story to the papers the moment Tristan left. He had to be extremely careful, so his choices were limited. He supposed he could fuck men who had as much to lose as him if they were outed—he knew a few players who were almost certainly gay—but the risk was twice as high. Or maybe he was just being paranoid.

Either way, hooking up with men was always too risky. That was why he mostly stuck to flirting with men and fucking women. Sex with women was unsatisfying at best and vaguely gross at worst, but it was safer. Smarter. He wasn't as stupid as Gabe to risk his career for a cock. It wasn't worth it.

But sometimes, the desire to feel a hard body against his own became too much and Tristan had little choice but to scratch the itch: sexual frustration made him snappish and bitchy, which was something he couldn't afford.

It was far harder to be a good, nice guy when all he wanted was a hard, rough fuck to relax. And when he wanted a hard fuck, his choices were very limited.

That was why Tristan was here.

The club was dark and foggy, with the distinctive smell of sweat and sex. There were lights on the stage, which were the first thing to catch the eye as he entered. The stage on the right was currently empty, but the one on the left was occupied by a naked brunette, who was flogging a stunning blonde. Strobe lights sparsely lit the large, crowded room, barely allowing him to make out individuals grouped in twos or threes—or more. It was one big orgy. The stench of sweat, sex and alcohol drenched the room, seeping into everything. Several rows of couches lined the walls, but Tristan didn't bother watching the occupants of them.

As he made his way through the club, numerous hands groped and petted him, trying to pull him closer. Grimacing, Tristan shrugged the hands off. He'd never been into orgies. He was bad at sharing; he always had been, even when he was a kid. But to be honest, that was just one of the reasons. The truth was, he couldn't quite suppress the uneasy feeling in his gut every time so many strangers touched him. No matter how many times Tristan told himself it was safe enough here, it was an exercise in futility.

Some habits never died. He was used to taking care of himself from a very young age, and back then, every stranger was dangerous. Even after he was adopted, things hadn't changed much. The DuVals had been kind people, forever involved in charity causes and volunteering work, but they had little clue what to do with a child and were more than happy to leave him—and later Gabriel—to his own devices. Tristan had been fine with it. Relying on other people was silly; he had always known that. He was on his own, as usual.

"Looking for someone?" a husky male voice said, grabbing his arm. "Maybe me?"

Tristan stopped and squinted at the man in the semi-darkness. Although he couldn't see him all that well, the guy seemed fairly attractive and didn't seem like a creep. Just a normal, horny guy looking for an anonymous fuck. He wasn't much taller than Tristan, but the hand on his arm was big and strong.

"You'll do," Tristan said. "I have a very strict condom policy. No bodily fluids."

The guy laughed, pulling him closer. "Don't worry, me too." His hands moved down Tristan's body, feeling him up. "Nice," he murmured, sliding his hands under Tristan's pants and kneading his cheeks. "You wanna blow me or—"

"Fuck me," Tristan said.

"Okay, I can definitely do that," the guy said with a chuckle, turning him to the wall and starting to work on his belt.

Tristan pressed his forehead against the cool wall and closed his eyes. He took a deep breath and tried to relax, but the persistent arousal that had been buzzing under his skin for the last few days was absent. Instead, he felt...uneasy, like he was doing something wrong.

"Absolutely not." Zach's eyes, hard and steely. "Sex is off-limits."

Tristan shifted from one foot to the other, trying to force the memory out of his mind. He wasn't going to obey

Zach's orders, like—like a good little boy. He wasn't.

He wouldn't.

His pants were being pulled down—

"Hey, what—" The guy made a startled noise. "What the hell, mate? Find someone else, I'm not sharing!"

"Sod off."

Tristan's eyes snapped open, his pulse skyrocketing. Zach. It was Zach.

"Whoa, easy there! Okay, I get it." The guy stalked off.

Slowly, Tristan turned around.

He could barely make out Zach's features in the semi-darkness, but he didn't need to see his face well to feel the anger emanating from every rigid movement of his body, see it in his set jaw.

"Are you stalking me?" Tristan said, zipping up his pants.

Zach said nothing. He merely grabbed Tristan's wrist, his grip like an iron band, and dragged him toward the exit.

His breath coming in harsh gasps, Tristan stumbled after him.

"Are you stalking me?" he asked again once they were outside.

Zach remained silent, dragging him toward his car.

He opened the door, shoved Tristan inside, got in the driver's seat and then they were off.

After a few minutes of charged, angry silence, Tristan crossed his arms over his chest. "Cat got your tongue?"

Zach said nothing, his eyes on the road. He was so tense it was making Tristan squirm a little.

"You won't make me feel guilty," Tristan said. He hated how defensive he sounded. "I did nothing wrong."

Silence.

Tristan gritted his teeth. "And what do you think you're doing, anyway? Don't you have better things to do than stalk your patients at night?"

"Not when those patients are spoiled idiots who can't take 'no' for an answer. I knew you'd do something stupid."

"What I do in my free time is none of your business," Tristan said.

"It is my business when you might fuck up your injury." Zach's voice could have cut glass. "I tell you to lay off sex, and a few hours later, I find you in a seedy sex club, with your pants around your ankles, ready to let some unwashed stranger fuck you and mess up all *my* work."

"I just wanted sex. It's not a crime to want sex. If I want to get laid, I damn well will!"

"You aren't allowed to have sex unless I say so."

Tristan blinked. "Excuse me?"

Zach didn't speak immediately, his gaze fixed straight ahead. "You wouldn't know when it's okay for you to have sex. That's why you can have sex only after I tell you it's okay."

Tristan's eyes bored into him. Zach's words were reasonable enough. But…

"Despite what you think, I'm not an idiot," Tristan said, watching his personal trainer carefully. He couldn't see him all that well in the semi-darkness. "If I'm not the one who does all the work during sex, it should be okay. I wouldn't have re-injured my groin in the position I was."

A muscle in Zach's jaw pulsed.

"Last time I checked, you weren't a physiotherapist."

Narrowing his eyes, Tristan studied him. The nagging feeling that something was off about Zach's behavior remained, but he didn't push.

"Aren't you surprised to find me in a gay sex club?" he asked instead. He should have probably been more bothered by this. A part of him waited for the panic to come—his sexuality was a carefully guarded secret—but he was oddly unconcerned.

Zach just scoffed.

"What?" Tristan said.

"I knew from the first day. I would have had to be blind not to notice."

"Notice what?" Tristan said, a stone of anxiety settling in his gut. Was he really obvious? "How did you know?"

Zach kept driving in silence.

"Notice what?" Tristan repeated, harder. "Zach!"

"You have that come-hither look in your eyes," Zach said irritably. "All the bloody time. Even when you're being a dick."

Tristan opened his mouth and closed it.

Glancing at him, Zach chuckled without much humor. "Don't tell me you're surprised. You look that way at everyone. Now stop changing the subject. You will promise me you won't do anything so stupid again. When I say no sex, I mean it."

"You were clearly born in the wrong century," Tristan said. "Sorry, but I'm not your little slave, and you can't throw me in the stocks for disobedience. You're forgetting yourself, Hardaway."

Zach swerved the car to the right, off the road, and slammed on the brakes; the tires screeched as the car came to a halt.

Tristan glanced around. They weren't far from his neighborhood. At this hour, this neighborhood was dark and relatively quiet.

"Let me get this straight," Zach said through his teeth, grabbing Tristan's chin roughly. "I'm responsible for your recovery, but you ignored my instructions *again* and risked fucking your groin up, and *I'm* forgetting myself?"

Tristan wet his lips with his tongue. There was something unnerving and exciting about Zach tonight, just like yesterday, when Zach got far more worked up than the situation had called for.

"Do you do everything to spite me, brat?" Zach said, in a soft voice that completely contradicted the punishing grip on Tristan's chin.

"Not everything is about you," Tristan said, just as softly. "I wanted a fuck. I wanted a nice, thick cock in me. I went out to get it. And I'll do it again. There's nothing you can do to stop me."

Zach sucked a breath in. He opened the door, grabbed Tristan's shoulder and hauled him over his knees. It happened so fast that Tristan could only splutter and gasp as he found himself flung over Zach's lap, his head sticking out of the car. "What—"

Zach jerked down Tristan's pants and briefs, and delivered a swift smack.

Tristan's eyes widened, his face flushing with outrage. "Let go!" He bucked, trying to roll off Zach's lap, but Zach was holding him firmly in place.

"I'm injured, you imbecile! What sort of therapist are you?"

"If you're fit enough for fucking, you're fit enough for spanking," Zach bit off.

"Maybe it'll finally teach you a lesson." He smacked him again. In this position, it didn't hurt his groin at all, but still. It was the principle of the thing.

"You'll be sacked for this—I'll tell Jared!"

"Do it." Another swat landed on his buttock.

"I'm serious, Hardaway. You'll be fired first thing in the morning! Even Jared won't object when he hears of this."

"Go run and complain to Jared," Zach said, smacking him again. His voice sounded harsh and odd. "You're nothing but a spoiled, self-centered little boy used to always getting his own way. If you keep being an unreasonable child, you'll be punished as a child would be."

"Screw you!" Tristan thrashed again, but Zach ignored it, keeping him down with one hand while the other spanked him. The spanking hurt but nowhere near as much as it could have: Zach was clearly holding back, mindful of his injury even now.

Another smack, and then another.

His skin began to burn a little and Tristan heard himself whimpering and moaning softly, his world narrowing down to Zach's hand and its heat. He felt strange, like he was floating, like he was floating around inside his body rather than wearing it, not a care in the world.

By the time Zach stopped, Tristan lay still and pliant over his lap.

Everything was eerily silent, save for Zach's harsh breathing and the distant sound of traffic.

The weight of Zach's hand on his bare skin felt almost unbearable. Tristan tried to say something scathing, but nothing came to mind. His mind was empty. He had no energy or inclination to bicker and fight. His body felt…loose. Floaty. He didn't want to move.

"Tristan?" Zach said after a long silence. His voice sounded strange.

Gently, he pulled Tristan's briefs and pants up and turned him onto his back.

He could barely make out Zach's face. He was glad, because he wasn't sure what his own face would have revealed. He wasn't even sure what he was feeling. Silently, Tristan scrambled off Zach's lap and dropped back into his seat. He closed his eyes, pressing his hot cheek against the cool leather.

After what felt like an eternity, the door closed.

The engine roared.

The car started moving.

Tristan didn't say a word.

Zach didn't say a word, either.

When the car stopped again, Zach said, "Your place." His voice was rough, uncomfortable, and yet there was something else there…something dark and intense.

Tristan didn't move. Didn't want to.

Seconds passed by in silence.

"That was highly unprofessional," Zach said after a while, his voice stiff, clipped. "I don't know what I was thinking. It won't happen again, but you're free to complain to Jared if you want to. I'm sure he'll find you another physio."

Tristan opened his eyes, opened the door, and got out.

The tires screeched and the car bolted forward.

Tristan walked toward his house slowly, his legs still a little weak and shaky.

He unlocked the front door, went in and leaned against it heavily, his thoughts in disarray.

And then it hit him: he really could get Zach fired. Finally, he had an excellent reason to get him sacked. Jared would be appalled if he found out what Zach had done: spanking a patient was beyond unprofessional.

He could get Zach fired.

He could get rid of him forever. No more lectures, no more of that high-handed attitude—and definitely no more spankings that left him feeling weird all over.

No more Zach.

Tristan's brows furrowed.

Chapter 5

"Why do you keep looking at your phone?"

Tristan lifted his gaze and found Lydia watching him.

"Zach is late today," he said. "You know I hate it when people make me wait."

Her brown eyes studied him curiously.

"What?" Tristan said, fiddling with his phone.

"What's going on with you and Zach lately?"

"I have no idea what you're talking about."

"I don't know…Something has changed."

Tristan gave her a pointed look. "Are you finished going through my mail? I don't pay you for twiddling your thumbs."

Visibly swallowing whatever snide remark she wanted to make, Lydia returned her eyes to the pile of envelopes in front of her.

Tristan looked back at his phone.

She was right, though. Something had changed.

Zach had been…different. He no longer tried to control every aspect of Tristan's recovery—and life. Zach left as soon as possible after checking Tristan's groin and giving him instructions for the day. Even his attitude had changed. Zach no longer called him "little boy," "baby," or "brat." There were no more wry smirks and jokes. In fact, his tone was neutral and extremely professional every time he spoke to Tristan.

And every time, Tristan wanted to punch him in the mouth.

Zach's oh-so-correct behavior drove him crazy. It annoyed him far more than Tristan had expected. And it didn't help that he was still horny and frustrated as hell. At least he had stopped feeling mortified when he got an erection while Zach massaged him. Because even seeing his erection got absolutely no reaction from Zach, not even a quirk of an eyebrow. Zach was professional to a T. Looking at Zach's behavior in the last ten days, it was hard to believe the spanking incident had ever happened.

Tristan squirmed a little. They hadn't talked about it, so the incident might as well have never happened. He hadn't told Jared anything. He still wasn't sure why.

"I like Zach," Lydia said suddenly. "He's such a nice guy. He invited me to his wedding."

Tristan's gaze snapped to her. "What? You've only known him for a few weeks."

Lydia gave him a very sweet smile. "You mean he didn't invite you?"

Tristan smiled back. Lydia was a bitch. She was fun, but she wasn't in his league when it came to bitchiness.

"I wouldn't have accepted the invitation, anyway," he said with perfect calmness. "Why would I want to go?"

Clearly disappointed, Lydia went back to sorting through his mail.

Tristan put the phone down before picking it up again. He stared at it for a moment.

"Have you seen his girlfriend?" he said casually.

"Donna? Oh yeah, she picked him up the other day when his car had broken down. He introduced us."

"What is she like?"

He felt her speculative gaze on him.

Keeping his face vaguely bored, Tristan said, "I'm curious what kind of woman would be stupid enough to marry such a bossy guy. She must be a doormat."

"She isn't," Lydia said immediately. "She's strong. It was obvious to me their relationship is that of equals. He respects her. She seemed practical and open-minded."

Tristan looked at his nails. "Do they claim to be in love?"

Lydia chuckled. "They're getting married, aren't they? They must be."

"Don't be silly. People get married all the time for many different reasons."

"Like what?"

"Habit," Tristan said. "Family expectations, financial reasons. Insecure people look for the security of marriage. Some people are afraid of being lonely. Some want kids. And so on and so forth. Love isn't necessary at all. Actually, accomplished people don't need to 'love' anyone to feel happy. Love is something people invented to excuse their idiotic behavior and to dress up lust with hearts and flowers."

"I hope one day you'll fall in love," Lydia muttered, barely audibly. "And that person will bring you to your knees."

Tristan smiled. "You're hilarious, sweetheart. That's why I keep you around, even though I know you hate my guts."

It was amusing to watch her face turn red. She opened and closed her mouth several times without saying anything.

At last, she cleared her throat. "Anyway, if you're waiting for Zach, don't. He isn't coming today."

Tristan's smile faded. "What?"

Lydia gave him an innocent look. "Didn't I tell you he called while you were in the shower? Oops. He told me he wasn't coming today. He said you knew what exercises to do. He has plans with Donna today."

Tristan stared at her.

Then, he called Zach.

"I don't remember giving you a day off," he said the moment Zach answered his phone.

"You don't need me today," Zach said. It sounded like he was driving. "You know what exercises you're supposed to do. You don't need me there to supervise you. You're not a child."

"I didn't give you a day off," Tristan said slowly, as though he was the one speaking to a small child. "You're my physiotherapist. You're supposed to check on my progress every day. You can't give yourself a day off whenever you want. What I want is the only thing that matters. Come here. Now."

"I'm busy, Tristan," Zach said. A female voice said something in the background.

Tristan's pulse started thudding in his ears. "I don't care. You will come here at once. As long as you are my therapist, I can keep you at my side for as long as it's necessary during your work hours. You signed the contract. Did you think I haven't read it? From nine in the morning till six in the evening, you're mine—if I want it. And now I want it."

"You're doing this just to spite me."

"You know me so well," Tristan said in his nicest voice. "Now get your behind over here."

Zach heaved a sigh. "Listen, b—Tristan. I'm really busy. I'm not alone. Give me a day off today, and tomorrow you can make me stick around the entire day doing nothing but watch you do nothing."

"I think not. I want you now." Tristan grimaced as soon as he said that, a rush of heat surfacing to his cheeks.

There was silence on the line.

"Spoiled baby," Zach said through his teeth.

Tristan felt an involuntary smile tug at his lips. "Always," he said and hung up, feeling ridiculously pleased by the fact that Zach had called him 'spoiled baby' and acted more like his old self.

Looking up, he found himself on the other end of Lydia's judgmental look. "What?"

Lydia shook her head. "It's just…you could have given him a day off. Do you know that he had freed his schedule up for the wedding? That's why Dr. Sheldon was able to hire him for you at all. If it weren't for this job, Zach would have been spending his time with his fiancée, as he had intended. As it should be."

"That's not my concern," Tristan said. "I'm injured. He's my physiotherapist. I need him here."

Lydia stared at him oddly but said nothing.

It was fifty-seven minutes before the doorbell rang.

Tristan didn't bother getting up from the couch. He waited, staring at the doorway, as Lydia went to open the front door.

The sound of footsteps and voices approached.

"Here he is," Lydia told Zach, rolling her eyes.

Zach walked over and simply stared him down for a long moment.

Finally, Zach spoke, "Can I talk to you for a minute, Tristan? Alone." Zach grabbed his wrist and none too gently dragged him out of the room.

Shutting the door, he turned to Tristan. "Well?" he said, his hand still gripping Tristan's wrist. "I'm here. Now what?"

Tristan pressed his lips together. "I don't know what you mean. You're supposed to be here, with me. You didn't even bother asking for my permission—and no, a call to Lydia doesn't fucking count."

"Donna has come home for only a few days between her work trips. I told you what exercises you must do today. You don't actually need me today."

"That's not the point," Tristan said. "You're my physio. You're supposed to be here if I want you here."

Zach raised his eyebrows. "And what do you want me here for? Hmm? To look at you while you lounge on the couch?"

Yes.

Tristan swallowed back the response that sprang to his lips. He didn't know where that had come from.

"Admit it," Zach said, taking Tristan's chin with his free hand. His gray eyes pierced into Tristan's. His thumb stroked behind Tristan's jaw and dug in, hard. "You don't need me here. You're just a spoiled little boy, and you've spoiled my day just because you could."

Tristan said with a smile, "Bite me."

Zach's eyes darkened. He lunged forward and bit Tristan's lip savagely.

They both froze. Their breathing meshed together.

A beat passed.

Tristan licked his lip and felt the copper taste of his own blood. Slowly, he lifted his eyes to meet Zach's.

Zach let go of him and stepped away, but Tristan grabbed a fistful of Zach's hair, yanked him close and bit his lip back. He gasped, feeling the bitter taste of blood and something purely male. He bit again.

Zach sucked a breath in before wrenching his mouth free.

They stared at each other, wide-eyed, their harsh breathing the only sound in the room.

At last, Zach turned away, but Tristan grabbed his biceps. Zach's muscles tensed up at his touch.

"You have blood on your lip," Tristan heard himself say. It felt distant, like a dream.

Zach didn't move to wipe the blood. His face was blank, but his eyes were frightening in their intensity as he stared at Tristan. He looked at Tristan like he was a venomous snake. A venomous snake he couldn't look away from.

Tristan leaned in and licked the blood on Zach's lip slowly—just his tongue against Zach's lip. Zach's body vibrated with tension against him—

Zach pushed him away and stalked out of the house.

As the front door slammed shut after him, Tristan closed his eyes. He breathed in and breathed out before opening his eyes again.

He gingerly touched his split lip and looked at his fingers.

They were shaking.

He curled them into a fist.

The door behind him opened.

"Is Zach gone already?" Lydia said, sounding bewildered.

Without a word, Tristan returned to the couch, pulled his knees to his chest, and wrapped his arms around them. He stared out the window.

"Tristan?"

"Get out," Tristan whispered.

"What?"

"Leave me alone."

Chapter 6

Jared called him just as he was getting ready for bed.

"What did you do this time, Tristan?"

"Hey, Jared," Tristan said, pulling his t-shirt off. He sat on the bed to remove his sock. "What are you talking about?"

"Zach called me and told me he wanted to quit."

Tristan paused. "Did he tell you why?"

"No. That's why I'm calling you."

Tristan removed the other sock. "What did you tell him?"

"That he's signed a contract and has to give me a good reason to break it." The disappointment in Jared's voice was unmistakable. "He's my friend, but he should know damn well that leaving patients in the middle of their recovery isn't okay without a good reason. Tell me what you did. Normally, Zach is very responsible and never gives up on his patients, no matter how difficult they are."

"Why are you assuming it was my fault?" Tristan stretched out on his back and looked at the ceiling.

"Are you saying you have nothing to do with it?" Jared said, his voice dry as sandpaper.

Tristan winced. Jared had said very little to him ever since his attempt to blackmail him. Once again, Tristan felt a pang of regret. He did like Jared. It was all Zach's fault. If Zach hadn't driven him mad, he would have thought twice before blackmailing the man who was going to be the senior club doctor in the foreseeable future. It had been rash of him.

"I'm not saying that." Tristan licked his lip. It no longer stung. "I'm saying that Zach is full of shit."

Jared heaved a sigh. "Look, I'm not going to pretend to understand what's going on with you two, but I'm tired of your constant fighting. Contract or not, if Zach really wants to quit, I can't force him to stay. He doesn't need this job, and he took it only as a favor for me. So sort it out, Tristan." Jared hung up.

Sort it out.

Tristan ran a hand over his face. It was easy for Jared to say. How was he supposed to do that when he didn't know what he wanted?

His lips curled. All right, fine—that was a lie. He did know what he wanted. Of course he did. He wanted Hardaway naked, on top of him and screwing him into the mattress.

A harsh laugh tore out of his throat.

The problem was, he didn't want to want it. It spelled trouble. It was reckless and stupid, and Tristan didn't do reckless and stupid.

For one thing, he didn't like Zach. He hated his holier-than-thou, superior attitude. Zach looked at him as if he had him figured out, as if he could see what a worthless piece of shit Tristan was.

To actually admit that he wanted Zach despite all of this—to actually act on those feelings (though lust had little to do with feelings)—was humiliating and cringe-worthy.

Admittedly, it probably was nowhere near as cringe-worthy as it must have been for Zach to want him against his better judgment.

Tristan smiled at the thought. There was something hilarious about the situation.

His smile slipped when he thought of another reason why this lust was very inconvenient. Zach was going to get married soon.

Tristan would be the first to admit he had very few moral principles, but there was one he never broke: he never got involved with a married man. He would never be so stupid. Besides, having an affair with one's very male personal trainer—a very well-known personal trainer— while said personal trainer was a few months away from marrying a sports journalist was a spectacularly bad idea. Potentially a career-ending idea. He wasn't an idiot to risk his career—his life—for a fuck with a man he disliked intensely. He wasn't. And even if he were, he'd never get involved with a married man, so the point was moot, anyway.

But god...Lusting after that prick was bad enough, but now that he knew that Zach wasn't as indifferent as he pretended, it was a recipe for disaster.

The thing was, Tristan had never been particularly good at denying himself things.

Chapter 7

Tristan knew who it was when the doorbell rang.

He opened the door and moved aside, letting Zach in.

Leaning back against the door, he regarded his guest in silence.

He'd never known silence could feel like that; never knew that it could have such a weight to it.

Zach's face was stony, his eyes glinting with an emotion Tristan couldn't quite place.

"Talk to Jared and tell him you agree with my decision to quit," Zach said. "Ask him to find you another personal trainer."

Tristan crossed his arms over his chest. That was what he had intended to do anyway, but Zach's uncompromising tone was rubbing him the wrong way. As usual.

"And why should I do that?" Tristan said. "Good morning to you, too, by the way."

A muscle twitched in Zach's jaw. "That's what you wanted. Do I need to remind you that you even tried to blackmail Jared to get rid of me?"

"Yes," Tristan said. "But maybe I changed my mind."
Stop it. What was he doing? He hadn't changed his mind. It was silly to antagonize Zach for the sake of antagonizing him.

But it was like his mouth was disconnected from his brain. There was no stopping it. "What are you doing here, anyway? If you want to quit, you don't need my permission. Sure, it would look bad on your CV, but—"

"Jared is my friend," Zach said. "I promised him I would help you, and I'd hate to let him down. He was pissed off when I refused to tell him why I wanted to quit. That's why you will tell him again that you want me gone."

"I will?" Tristan said softly. He put on a confused face. "By the way, why do you want to quit?"

He received such a glare, it made a shiver run up his spine. All of a sudden, he wanted to grin. Winding Zach up was one of his favorite things in the world.

"Don't play coy, Tristan," Zach said, his voice clipped. "You know why."

"I don't think so. And do you have to stand so far away?" Tristan was unable to suppress his grin any longer. "If I didn't know better, I'd think you were afraid."

If he hadn't been watching him so closely, he would have missed the stiffening of Zach's posture. Then he was stalking toward Tristan.

His heartbeat picking up, Tristan gripped the doorknob behind him.

Zach came to a halt just a few inches away.

Tristan exhaled, hating how shaky it sounded.

Zach took his chin and tilted it up, his fingers rough against the sensitive skin of Tristan's neck. His steely eyes bored into Tristan's. "I think you're confusing something, brat," he said, his lips curling into a familiar wry smile.

"I'm not afraid of you. I want to quit the job because you annoy me too much and I can't behave professionally around you. That's it."

"Ah," Tristan said, looking at him from under his eyelashes. "So you kissed me because you were annoyed. It makes so much sense now."

"I didn't kiss you," Zach all but gritted out. His body almost pressed against Tristan's. Almost.

"No, of course not," Tristan said. Someone was breathing hard; he hoped it wasn't him. "You just bit me. You bit my lip and let me lick yours."

Zach's Adam's apple moved. "You annoyed me."

"I don't know about you, but I don't bite people's lips when they annoy me." Tristan licked the corner of his dry mouth. They were so close now he could feel Zach's breath on his lips. "Are you annoyed at me now?" His voice came out all wrong: it was supposed to sound like a taunt, it was supposed to piss Zach off, but instead it sounded like an invitation. God, he was breathing and trembling like he was in the middle of sex and the only place Zach was touching was his neck! This was ridiculous.

"Why are you doing this?" Zach said hoarsely, glowering at him with glazed eyes. His fingers tightened around Tristan's neck. "You can't want this, either."

"I don't," Tristan agreed dazedly. "I don't want this." *Push him away. Kick him out.*

But he couldn't. He couldn't move. "I don't," he whispered again, his hand reaching up to bury in Zach's thick brown-gold hair. "This is all your fault." His shaking fingers dug into Zach's nape as Zach's lips almost brushed his. Zach's stubble scratched his chin. "I hate you," he murmured already into Zach's mouth—

And then they were kissing—if that could be called kissing at all, more like attacking. Zach *ravished* his mouth with wet, deep kisses, with a ferocious hunger that weakened Tristan's knees. In one quick shove Zach had him pinned, trapped between the door, his hard body, and Tristan's own desperate, pressing need. God. Zach's tongue plunged into his mouth, sweeping inside and plundering, owning, and Tristan was kissing him back, heedless of the sharp metallic tang of blood that mingled on their tongues. The flames that were burning in his blood erupted into a sudden inferno, and he was lost, only distantly aware that he was gasping and grinding helplessly against Zach's hip, his hand fisted in Zach's shirt and his mind blissfully empty beyond a formless depth of want, and desire, and carnal need. So much need.

Moaning into Zach's mouth, Tristan slid his hand between them and grabbed the bulge in Zach's pants. Zach shuddered and bit his lip with a groan, his cock pushing against Tristan's greedy hand. God, he wanted this. Wanted it in, deep and hard.

"Fuck me," he heard himself beg. Was it really his voice, shaky and pathetic? "Please fuck me."

Everything stopped. The kisses stopped. Zach went rigid.

Zach tore his mouth away, his chest heaving, his eyes stormy. "No." He all but shoved Tristan away from the door and then he was gone.

His knees buckling, Tristan slid down to the floor and closed his eyes, trying to ignore the shivers of want still racking his body. Anger, embarrassment and humiliation burned at his insides.

Stupid, stupid, *stupid*.

Chapter 8

When Tristan was five, his mother took him to a big house in the suburbs of London.

Memory was such a fickle thing. Tristan didn't remember a lot of things that happened more recently, but he did remember that cold, rainy evening with perfect clarity. He remembered the chill seeping into his small body as he stood, clutching his mother's thin hand. She was shivering, her grip on his hand painful. Tristan thought she was scared. He was scared, too.

"I'm cold," he complained.

"Hush. You'll be warm soon," she said before coughing violently. She let go of his hand to cover her mouth. She always did it, as if he couldn't hear. As if he was stupid.

Tristan averted his gaze for the minute it took before her coughs subsided and the sound of her breathing became less scary. A gust of wind blew into his face, almost knocking him off his feet and temporarily blurring his vision.

He hated this.

"I wanna go home," he muttered, even though he hated their home: the tiny, cold room that was crawling with things.

Sighing, his mother turned and leaned down so they were eye to eye. Her face was gray, thin and ugly, her eyes dull with pain. Tristan hated her face, too. She used to look so different. She used to be the most beautiful woman in their neighborhood. The illness made her ugly and Tristan hated it and hated her.

"Baby," she said hoarsely. "Remember you used to ask about your dad? This is his home—one of his homes. You're going to live with him now."

Tristan's eyes widened. He glanced at the big house. "Dad?"

"Yes," she said, taking his hand again and pulling him toward the house. "He's—he's a very important person and he can give you anything you need. He'll—he'll take care of you."

As her words sank in, Tristan snatched his hand away and ran ahead of her. A dad. *His* dad! Billy had a dad. Tom had a dad too. Even that stupid Charlie Kane had a dad. A dad. He had a real dad. And maybe his dad would fix whatever was wrong with his mom, too!

Tristan banged on the front door.

"Tris—" his mother admonished, but a terrible coughing fit interrupted anything else she was going to say.

The door opened, revealing a man on the other side.

He wasn't very tall, but he looked…nice. He didn't look like Tristan—everyone said Tristan looked like his mother—but he had eyes just like him.

The man—*his dad*—stared at him in confusion, a polite smile on his lips.

Tristan heart thumped in his chest. He smiled. "Hello."

"Hello," his dad said gently. "Can I help you, young man?"

Tristan beamed at him. "I'm Tristan."

Looking puzzled, his dad glanced over Tristan's shoulder.

Behind Tristan, his mother finally stopped coughing.

"Hello, Arthur," she said, her voice still terrible from coughing.

His dad stared at her, his face…empty.

As the silence stretched on, Tristan got a funny feeling in his stomach.

"I'm sorry, sir, I didn't hear the knocking," an apologetic male voice said suddenly. "You shouldn't be answering the door."

"That's all right, David," his dad said after a moment. "It's no one important. You may go."

Tristan frowned. Maybe he just hadn't recognized her? She looked so different now that she was…sick.

"I'm your son, Tristan," he tried again, trying to give the man his nicest smile. Billy's mother always said he was "a pretty child" and "irresistible" when he was nice.

His dad gave him a very strange look.

Before he could say anything, there was the sound of someone running, and then, a blond boy, about Tristan's age, came crashing into Tristan's dad's legs. "Daddy, we didn't finish playing!" he said, grabbing the man's hand and tugging.

"Wait for me in the living room, James."

The boy glanced at Tristan and made a face. "Give the beggars something and let's go!"

Tristan glared at the boy, suddenly painfully aware that he did look like a beggar compared to the boy, who was wearing neat and clean clothes. Tristan had never even seen clothes like that. "Take it back!" he said, lunging forward and pushing the boy. "I'm not a beggar!"

"Tristan—" his mother started, but another coughing fit interrupted her halfway through.

"Dad!" the boy cried out, trying to push Tristan away.

Hands grabbed Tristan's collar and pushed him away from the boy.

Looking up, Tristan met his dad's angry eyes. He got that funny feeling in his stomach again.

"Tell him I'm not a beggar," he whispered. "Tell him I'm your son."

Something flickered in his dad's eyes, something like hesitation. He looked over Tristan's shoulder at his mother.

"Arthur, please," she said, her voice breaking. "He has no one. When I go, he…"

"Daddy, who are these people?" the boy whined.

"Arthur?" a cultured female voice called out. There was the sound of approaching footsteps. "Who is it?"

Swallowing, his father let go of Tristan's collar.

"No one," he said and shut the door in Tristan's face.

Memory was a fickle thing. Tristan didn't remember what he told his mother afterward or what she said to him. He had only a vague memory of his mother's death a few months later. But he remembered with perfect clarity what he felt as he stared at that pristine white door sixteen years ago: the feeling of inadequacy and utter humiliation and hurt. And anger.

Lots and lots of anger.

Tristan shook his head with a crooked smile.

God, this was so pathetic.

He was perfectly aware what a textbook case he was. Freud would have had a field day with him. He knew that one of the reasons he couldn't stand Gabriel was because he projected his hatred for the boy—his real brother—onto him, though it didn't help that Gabriel often made him feel inferior, too.

Gabriel often accused him of being a two-faced, manipulative shit. He wasn't wrong. But he wasn't right, either. Tristan would have liked to be as devious as Gabe imagined him to be, but the truth was simpler and far more demeaning: Tristan made so much effort to be liked by other people because he needed it.

But being aware of his problems and actually doing something about them were two different things. It had been sixteen years and he still couldn't deal with rejection any better than he had when he was a child. He hated feeling inadequate. Inferior. Unwanted and humiliated.

He'd never hated Zach Hardaway more.

Tristan closed his eyes, trying to clear his mind, but he couldn't erase the memory of his own shaky, needy voice begging Zach and the slap of rejection. Of course Zach had rejected him—he might have wanted Tristan physically, but he had a perfect little girlfriend he was marrying.

Tristan's father would have approved.

A laugh bubbled up his throat and Tristan shook his head. No. He wouldn't let Zach reduce him to this. He wasn't going to wallow in self-pity. So Zach rejected him; so what? It was a good thing. It didn't matter how humiliating it was—it *was* a good thing that Zach had stopped before they could go too far. If he had slept with Zach, he would have regretted it, anyway. A fuck wasn't worth his self-esteem. He would never be the "other woman," as his mother had been. So screw Zach.

Tristan didn't give a damn about him. He was Tristan DuVal, a world-class football star and millionaire, and he was awesome. Millions of people wanted to be him. Millions wanted him. Zach was nothing. Zach was no one to him. Zach didn't deserve to kiss his boots. And Zach sure as hell didn't deserve an easy way out.

His jaw set, Tristan pulled his phone out and called him.

"Look," Zach said when he finally answered. "About what happened—"

"You've neglected your job for two days," Tristan cut him off, his voice hard. "I expect you to be here first thing in the morning."

There was silence on the line.

At last, Zach said, "I'm on my way to Jared. I'm handing in my notice."

"Why?" Tristan said.

Zach exhaled audibly. "Tris—"

"No, I really don't get why you're quitting the job." Tristan scoffed, making sure to sound as derisive as possible. "If it's about what happened this morning, forget about it. Obviously it won't happen again. I don't know what I was thinking." Tristan smiled grimly, pleased with how bored and indifferent his voice sounded. "I expect to see you here tomorrow."

"I'm quitting, Tristan."

"Ah, I get it," he said amiably. "You're scared that you won't be able to keep your hands off me."

"I'm not scared of that," Zach said testily.

"Then prove it," Tristan said softly. "But I think you can't. You're afraid to be around me."

"How do you get into your front door with a head so big?" Zach asked with a laugh.

"It's a special talent. I'm very talented. Don't be late."
Tristan hung up, knowing that he had won.

Or lost, something whispered in the back of his mind.

The truth was, he was scared, too.

Chapter 9

When the doorbell rang the next morning, Tristan was already in the gym, stretching his muscles before his training session.

He didn't hurry to the door—he stopped to check his reflection in the mirror.

Tristan ran his hand through his brown hair, making his already messy hair even more disheveled. He glanced at his clothes: a tank top that made his eyes look blue rather than green and a pair of white shorts that showed off his legs and ass to perfection.

Tristan smiled grimly. Perfect. He wanted Zach to stare at him, knowing that he could never, ever have him.

The doorbell rang again. Someone was getting impatient.

With one final glance at the mirror, Tristan went to open the door.

Zach's eyes immediately went to Tristan's hips and legs. His lips thinned. He shoved his hands into the pockets of his jacket and gave Tristan a very unimpressed look.

Tristan smiled innocently. "Good morning."

Still saying nothing, Zach continued boring a hole in Tristan with his eyes.

Tristan licked his dry lips and cleared his throat.

"Okay, I want to make something clear: what happened yesterday was moronic and will never happen again. You kiss terribly, by the way."

"Do I?" Zach said through his teeth, still looking pissed off. "I got a different impression yesterday."

Tristan glared at him. "I'll have you know I just have a very sensitive mouth. I enjoy having something in my mouth, that's all."

Zach stared at him.

Tristan fought back the blush threatening to creep up his cheeks, wondering what the hell was wrong with him. His brain-to-mouth filter seemed non-existent when Zach was around.

Figuring offense was the best defense, Tristan smiled. "You're imagining my mouth around your dick, admit it."

Zach's jaw worked.

"Don't bother denying it," Tristan said with a shrug. "I don't care. It's not like it would ever happen, so you can imagine all you want. You'll never touch me again."

"Don't be absurd," Zach said. "I'm your physiotherapist. I can't avoid touching you."

Feeling silly and embarrassed—he felt that way far too often in Zach's presence—Tristan glowered and headed to the gym, trying not to stomp, mindful of his injury. His groin didn't bother him at all lately, but he wasn't willing to risk re-injury— he would never hear the end of it from Zach.

"Stop swinging your hips," Zach said irritably, following him.

"No one's forcing you to look," Tristan said, just as irritably.

Bloody hell, this had been a terrible idea. He shouldn't have manipulated Zach into staying simply because his pride was wounded. What was he trying to prove? It was obvious they couldn't achieve a working relationship while this…thing was hanging between them, taut and loaded. God, he'd never before wanted sex so badly that he had to consciously stop himself from jumping the guy's bones.

They entered the gym in tense silence and looked at each other.

Zach moved toward the mats. "Did you do your exercises yesterday?" His voice was cool and very professional all of a sudden. "Hip adduction, hip flexion?"

"Yeah," Tristan said.

"Isometric adductor exercises?"

"Yeah."

"Did you apply ice after the exercises?"

"Of course I did."

"Any pain?"

Tristan shook his head.

"No soreness now?"

"I told you I'm ready for training. Real training."

"I will be the judge of that," Zach said, leaning against the wall and crossing his arms over his chest. "Start. Stretching first."

Rolling his eyes, Tristan grabbed the medicine ball. "Already did."

He did his exercises in silence, trying to ignore the black-clad figure watching him like a hawk. He didn't look Zach's way, but he could feel his heavy gaze, almost like a physical touch.

He felt Zach's gaze as he reclined on his back and spread his legs. As he bent his knees and placed his feet flat on the floor. As he placed the medicine ball between his knees and pressed inward. He felt Zach's gaze on his legs and thighs as they strained and squeezed. He was suddenly acutely aware of how truly tiny his shorts were. And although he had dressed this way to drive Zach crazy, now it was coming to bite him in the ass. He felt naked and overstimulated.

"Stop staring at me," Tristan said, turning on his side to do hip adduction against gravity.

"I'm not staring at you. I'm observing. That's my job."

Tristan snorted, bending the top leg over to the front of his lower leg. He lifted the lower leg as high as possible, panting a little as he held it up. "I'm pretty sure your job doesn't involve ogling your patient's thighs."

Zach laughed. "You have a rich imagination. You see only what you want to see."

Tristan rolled onto his back and looked up at him. "What is that supposed to mean?"

Zach walked over and knelt down by Tristan's feet. "Eccentric adduction now," he said, instead of responding. His eyes were downcast and his face was difficult to read. "Legs out straight."

"Stop changing the subject," Tristan said, but he did as he was told. "If you have something to say, say it. What are you implying here?"

Zach's hand wrapped around his ankle. "I will move your leg out to the side and you must resist the movement but not so much that the leg doesn't move. Understood?"

His big fingers brushed the sensitive skin of his ankle. Tristan's toes curled. "Answer the goddamn question," he said.

Zach forcefully moved the leg out to the side and Tristan sucked a breath in—although Zach was relatively gentle, there was definitely some discomfort as Tristan tried to resist and slow down the movement.

"This exercise is a little more advanced," Zach said, as if Tristan hadn't said anything. "It's more likely to cause some muscle soreness tomorrow."

Tristan took a deep breath through his teeth. "I asked you a question."

"Don't ask questions you don't want to hear the answers to."

"Let me be the judge of that," Tristan said, knowing how much it irritated Zach when he threw his own words back at him.

Finally, Zach looked him in the eye. The crooked smile on his lips was at odds with the intense, dead serious look in his eyes. "If these shorts were any shorter, they'd be called belts. I've never seen a more obvious come-on than what you're wearing today."

Struggling to keep his expression under control, Tristan managed to put on a sassy smirk. "I think you're the one who sees what he wants to see. I hate to break it to you, but I don't want you. I'm not trying to—to seduce you, or something. If I were, you'd already be flat on your back, begging me."

"You sure it's not the other way around?" Zach murmured, a glimmer of amusement in his eyes. "I remember it differently."

Ugh, Tristan had never wanted to kill anyone more.

He lifted his chin. "That was a moment of madness."

"That I agree with," Zach said. "I'm straight."

Tristan's eyebrows crawled up. "I got a different impression yesterday."

"As you said, that was a moment of madness. I'm not interested in men."

"Really?" Tristan said, grinning. "Then it must have been your evil gay twin whose tongue was down my throat yesterday. Does your future wife know about it?"

Zach met his eyes calmly. "I've already told you, Donna and I are in an open relationship until the wedding. And for someone who keeps saying it was a mistake, you sure keep talking about it a lot."

Tristan searched for something to say—something that would give him the upper hand, something that would stop him from feeling so out of his depth. The sardonic curl of Zach's lips was absolutely infuriating. Zach knew Tristan wanted him, and after yesterday's humiliation, Tristan could hardly deny it.

But why should he deny it?

"The truth is, I was just horny," Tristan said and smiled at Zach. "Yep, you can add 'slut' to the long list of my flaws. I was horny and you were just there. The truth is, any dick would do."

Zach's fingers tightened around Tristan's ankle.

Tristan cocked his head, looking at him innocently. "What? Don't tell me you thought you were special. If I weren't injured, I'd be getting laid every night." The blatant lie rolled off his tongue easily. "But I get it: of course you'd like to think I'm into you—anyone would. I'm irresistible."

"Irresistible isn't the word I would use to describe you." Zach's grip on his ankle was almost painful now.

"Lovely?" Tristan said with a grin, batting his eyelashes. Goading Zach was always so fun. "Beautiful? Fuckable?"

Zach's glare was strong enough to send someone cowering away. "Spankable."

"Ah," Tristan said, struggling to keep his tone light-hearted and mocking. "Admit it: you totally loved spanking me. You're dying to do it again." He meant it as a joke. Mostly.

But when Zach's eyes *glazed*, Tristan's smile faded, his mouth suddenly very dry.

Their eyes locked.

Move, the voice in the back of his mind whispered. *Get out of here.*

But Tristan couldn't, pinned by Zach's gaze and caught in a web of need.

Every passing second made each breath more and more difficult, leaving Tristan feeling oddly exposed and vulnerable. But it was a double-edged sword: he knew Zach wanted it, too.

"Come here," Zach said, his voice low-pitched and his face grim.

It was vague, but Tristan knew what he meant. What they both wanted.

Slowly, as though in a dream, Tristan moved and laid himself over Zach's lap. Burying his face in the mat, he closed his eyes as he felt Zach's hand tug his shorts down, his movements impatient, urgent and jerky.

He was wearing no underwear. Tristan could almost physically feel Zach's eyes on the curve of his bare ass.

They probably shouldn't do this.

But on the other hand, this was safe enough. It wasn't sex, but it was *something*. An outlet for all the pent-up frustration that had been building up within him.

A slap landed on his cheek.

Tristan swallowed the gasp that rose to his lips. He could feel the sting and the residual heat where Zach's hand had landed.

It felt…weird: satisfying at the same time as it was humiliating. Which probably only went to prove that he was out of his mind to have ever let himself get into this situation.

For a long moment, Zach's hand merely caressed the smooth skin that still bore the imprint of his fingers.

Tristan tried to fight the temptation to move his hips and lean into the touch. It wasn't sex. They weren't having sex. "That's all you've got? Feels like a bee sting."

"You little—" Zach's hand came down on his buttock in a hard, stinging slap. Tristan gasped, rubbing his flushed cheek against the mat as Zach began spanking him in earnest, not giving him any time to talk between blows.

This time Tristan didn't fight the floaty, warm feeling that started clouding his senses. He relaxed, gasping with every smack. His skin began to sting pretty hard, and every smack felt sharper and *better*—

Suddenly, the spanking stopped. Tristan made a disappointed noise.

"If I don't stop now, you won't be able to sit tomorrow," Zach said, his voice harsh and his breath ragged.

Tristan squirmed against Zach's palm. More.

"It will hurt," Zach grunted, his big hand touching Tristan's stinging cheek.

Tristan squirmed again, leaning into the touch. He couldn't ask aloud.

"It will be irresponsible." Zach sounded like he was trying to convince himself.

"Shut up and just do it," Tristan whispered. "Make me hurt."

Silence. The moment stretched out.

He could feel Zach looking down at him, and the tension mounted as Tristan resisted the urge to turn his head and meet Zach's eyes, to end this maddening waiting. He wanted to plead with Zach to spank him harder, to take him, to just *do* something—

He couldn't hide his gasp when a hand dug into his hair, forcing Tristan to turn his head and look at Zach. The heat in Zach's gray eyes burned him, the intensity making something inside of him turn warm. It felt like Zach's face filled his entire world, leaving room for nothing else. Zach's hand went to Tristan's throat, so gentle, yet so threatening. A thumb stroked his pulse before the fingers tightened, ever so slightly.

Tristan didn't move, just looked at him from under his eyelashes.

Zach's nostrils flared. He bent forward, bringing his face close to Tristan's, until their breath mingled and their lips were so close, so close…Tristan strained for the contact, aching for Zach's lips, wanting to be kissed, but Zach straightened up with a low, "Fuck." Tristan couldn't quite stifle the whine of disappointment.

Zach looked at him, a dark expression on his face.

Suddenly Tristan was painfully aware how vulnerable he was in this position: lying half-naked across his physio's lap, with absolutely no leverage to do anything. And Zach's hand was still around his throat.

Looking Zach in the eye, Tristan relaxed, baring his throat further.

Zach inhaled sharply, lunged forward and sank his teeth into the sensitive skin of Tristan's neck. They both moaned, and Tristan's eyes slid close, his body going slack, his mind blissfully blank as Zach practically *chewed* on his neck. It wasn't a kiss, nor was it a hickey. It hurt—it hurt a great deal, but the pain mixed with such toe-curling pleasure that Tristan found himself grinding his erection against Zach's thigh.

"You aren't supposed to be enjoying this." A vicious whack landed on his left buttock, the force of it making air whoosh past his lips, and then another, and another. All the while Zach kept sucking and biting on his neck, his harsh breath the only sound Tristan could focus on.

He had no idea how long it lasted. Everything was a blur of pain and pleasure and his moans and Zach's heavy breathing and teeth. His eyes were wet but he couldn't bring himself to care. There was another swat, and another, until his skin was burning and Tristan was squirming, wanting, needing—

"Zach—" he breathed out, mouth dry like sandpaper.

Zach's firm lips moved up his neck, stubble scratching Tristan's skin, before his teeth sank into Tristan's earlobe and a smack landed right between his cheeks. Tristan cried out, coming hard, and then he was drowning, and he wanted nothing more than to melt into Zach, plummeting into the warm, quiet haze. He let out a small, desperate sound, needing—

He sighed when Zach stretched out next to him, pulling him to his shoulder. A warm hand settled on his nape, somehow steadying him, and Tristan floated away, feeling safe, and calm, and warm. So warm.

Before he knew it, he was asleep.

Chapter 10

Tristan stared at his reflection in the mirror. At the handprints on his ass. At his neck that made him look like he was a victim of a vampire. He had told Lydia to reschedule the interview he was supposed to give that afternoon. He could hardly give interviews when he looked like this.

Biting his lip, Tristan touched the giant hickey on the side of his neck and shivered. Despite the evidence, it all seemed pretty surreal. When he had woken up in the gym yesterday, there was no trace of Zach in the house. Tristan would have thought it was just a very vivid, freaky dream if it hadn't felt like his buttocks were on fire and he didn't have dried come on his skin.

He wondered if Zach would even come this morning. He doubted it.

The doorbell rang.

Tristan's stomach plummeted into an icy hell somewhere below his boots.

He pulled his sweatpants up and hurried downstairs.

When he opened the door, Zach's eyes zeroed in on his throat. On the marks his teeth had left yesterday. Tristan suppressed the silly urge to cover them.

It felt like a small eternity passed before Zach looked him in the eye.

Tristan moistened his lips with his tongue, unsure what to say. Hell, he wasn't even sure what had *happened*. Strictly speaking, what happened yesterday wasn't sex; they didn't even kiss. Zach had just given him a spanking and a few nasty hickeys. So yeah, strictly speaking, it wasn't sex. But in some ways, it was worse. His memory was a bit hazy, but he was pretty sure he hadn't imagined Zach holding him afterward. Or had it been a dream? Looking at Zach now, it was hard to believe any of that had happened.

Tristan moved aside.

Zach entered the house, the very inflexibility of his movements speaking volumes. He was wound up tighter than a bowstring ready to snap.

Tristan shut the door and leaned against it, feeling a strong sense of deja-vu.

Unexpectedly, Zach leaned against the door, too. Tristan had thought that Zach would try to put as much distance between them as possible. And yet they stood close. Their shoulders were brushing.

Tristan hooked a thumb in the waistband of his sweatpants and caught his lip between his teeth. Despite the several layers of fabric, his skin was tingling where their shoulders were touching. Jesus. This thing was ridiculous.

At last, Zach heaved a sigh, breaking the silence. "I hate to repeat the obvious, but…"

"It was a mistake," Tristan said, looking at the opposite wall.

"Yes."

Another long, tense silence.

"Look," Zach said. "I don't want to be that guy. I'm not that guy."

"That guy?" Tristan smiled. "You mean the guy who's getting married in a few months, who says he's straight, and who says he doesn't like bullshit?"

"All of those things are true."

Tristan hummed. "You have a funny way of showing it. Why are you here?"

"What?"

Tristan turned his head to him and was a little taken aback by how close their faces were. "What are you doing here, Zach?" he asked in a low, soft voice. "If you're so disgusted by what happened, you should have gone straight to Jared and told him you were quitting. No one can force you to stay, contract or not." Tristan cocked his head. "So, what are you doing here?"

He studied Zach's profile as Zach stared in front of him. He could see the barely noticeable pulsing of the muscles in Zach's jaw.

Tristan placed a hand on Zach's biceps. The muscles went rigid as he slowly dragged his hand down Zach's arm to his wrist. He could feel the incredible tension in Zach's body, and it was mirrored in his own.

Tristan cringed when he realized that his fingers were shaking.

Shaking.

For fuck's sake.

"Don't touch me," Zach said, his voice strained.

"You know what I think?" Tristan murmured, his fingers wrapping around Zach's wrist. He clenched them so the tremor wasn't as noticeable.

"I think you hate it. Hate that you want me. You hate it and you think it's wrong—and gay—and that you can't possibly want someone you don't even like. You think you're better than that, but the thing is, you *aren't*. Or you wouldn't be here with me now."

Zach looked at him. "I don't want you."

Tristan touched his own neck. "Then what is this?"

Zach's eyes skimmed over the hickeys. His lips thinned into a line.

Tristan smiled cheekily. "Ah, I know! The evil twin strikes again? Or maybe—"

Zach slammed their mouths together. Moaning, Tristan grabbed Zach's hair and yanked him closer, opening his mouth, eager, so damn eager. God. Zach's lips were hot and rough, his scruff sending shivers down Tristan's spine. Zach's lips tasted of resentment, anger and something primitive. It was the deepest, wildest kiss he'd ever had. Zach kissed him like he both hated and craved it, his mouth like a branding iron, searing his lips and stirring his senses into a frenzy of heady desire and want. He wanted—needed—Zach's lips everywhere, all over his body, sucking on his neck, his nipples, his cock, between his cheeks…

As if reading his thoughts, Zach's mouth moved to his neck, nibbling and sucking. Tristan gasped, his eyes rolling to the back of his head. He should probably stop Zach— he'd never been a fan of people marking him—but he couldn't. *He wants me, he wants me, he wants me…*

Tristan dug his blunt nails into Zach's nape and whispered, "You want me."

Zach's mouth went still, his shoulders stiffening. He pulled away slowly.

Breathing hard, they looked at each other. Zach's pupils were so blown that his eyes seemed dark.

"No," he said, his voice barely recognizable. "I don't want you." He turned his face away, putting his hand on the doorknob. "This is not want."

Tristan took a deep, calming breath. At least it was supposed to be calming. "Then what is this?" Because it sure as hell felt like want. It felt like his body was on fire, his whole body alive like it had never been before. He *wanted* so badly that he was shaking with it, his balls and cock aching. He could barely stop himself from latching onto Zach again and begging him to take him, but the sting of rejection was still fresh in his mind. He'd be damned if he begged him again.

"Weakness," Zach said testily. "I don't want you. Not as a person."

"Ah," Tristan said. He tried to curl his lips into a smile. It was harder than usual. "You just want to screw me."

"I don't—" Zach said before cutting himself off. He clenched his jaw and glared at Tristan, as if it was somehow his fault.

Of course it was.

Tristan straightened up and moved away. "Don't worry, I get it: this is all my fault. I'm the bad guy, as usual. Get out, tell Jared you quit, and go back to your girlfriend." He headed upstairs, feeling Zach's gaze on his back.

At the top of the stairs, Tristan stopped and looked over his shoulder.

He smiled brightly. "Bye. Try not to think of me when you fuck her." Whistling a cheerful tune, he resumed walking.

Once he was in his room and out of Zach's sight, Tristan slumped against the door. There was an unpleasant, tight feeling lodged in his throat and he didn't know how to get rid of it.

I don't want you. Not as a person.

"I hate you," he whispered. "I hate you."

What was it about him that made him so unlo— unlikeable? Did people look into his eyes and see nothing worthy? Was he such a bad, unattractive person?

Maybe he was.

Blinking rapidly, Tristan walked over to the bed and flopped down. He hugged his pillow and closed his eyes.

"I don't care," he said aloud. He had never cared before. He wasn't going to start now.

He was Tristan DuVal, a football star, and he was—he was…

Everyone loved him. People loved him.

They loved him.

Chapter 11

Jared Sheldon leaned back in his chair and regarded his friend in silence.

Zach met his eyes steadily.

"So, you haven't changed your mind," Jared said. "You still want to quit."

"Yes."

"And you still refuse to tell me why," Jared said coldly. He wasn't exactly happy with Zach right now. Zach was the last person he'd expected to be so irresponsible and quit in the middle of his patient's rehabilitation process. And on a purely personal level, it pissed him off that Zach didn't trust him enough to share why he wanted to leave. They were good friends. At least, he had considered Zach one of his closest friends in England.

"Look," Zach said. The conflict on his face was easy to see. "It's...it's personal."

Jared stared at him. "Personal?"

Running a hand over his face, Zach pinched the bridge of his nose.

"I can't keep a professional distance. He gets under my skin."

That Jared could believe. The world knew Tristan as a likable, easy-going guy, but Jared had come to realize how erroneous that impression was. Still, he didn't believe that Tristan was the devil's spawn Gabriel painted him as.

Things were rarely black and white, bad guys and good guys.

"I thought you could handle him," Jared commented, watching Zach curiously. The last time he'd seen Zach and Tristan in the same room, Tristan was the one demanding he fire Zach, while Zach was cool and collected, even amused. What had changed?

"I thought so, too," Zach said, a corner of his mouth curling up in a humorless smile. "I'm used to difficult patients, you know that."

"But?"

"He's trying to seduce me."

At first he thought he had misheard Zach.

But of course he hadn't.

"Ah," Jared said. He chuckled. "Is that all? It's just the way he is. Tristan's always been a flirt."

The look on Zach's face was difficult to read.

"He came onto you?" he said. His voice was a little strange.

Jared frowned, looking at his friend appraisingly. Zach had never been homophobic. Zach's own younger brother was gay, and Zach had been nothing but supportive when Nick came out.

But there was definitely something off about his reaction.

"He used to flirt with me a lot, but it was nothing serious," Jared said slowly. "I thought he did it just for the fun of it and to annoy Gabriel."

"And you were never tempted?"

Laughing a little, Jared said, "I'm not a monk. He's easily the most gorgeous guy I've ever met."

Zach's eyes pierced into him like twin daggers.

Jared shook his head. "Nothing happened. He's my patient, Zach."

Something flickered across Zach's face. "Gabriel is your patient, too."

Jared paused, wondering how Zach knew about him and Gabe.

"It's different," he said. "You know how special he is to me.

Tristan is—yeah, he's ridiculously beautiful. I'm a healthy gay man and I have eyes, but I was never really attracted to him. I couldn't see him as anything but Gabriel's brother. When you already love someone, it's easy to control trivial lusts."

Zach flinched.

Jared studied the sudden tension in Zach's shoulders and the way his hand was balling into a fist. It was puzzling. He'd never seen his friend so agitated. It wasn't Zach's way.

Being the eldest in his family and used to managing his younger siblings, Zach wasn't one to get all wound up easily. Some people considered Zach overbearing, even arrogant, but Jared knew it was just the consequence of Zach being responsible for so many people ever since he was a teenager. If someone had asked Jared to describe Zach with one word, he would definitely pick the word "responsible." That was why Zach's sudden decision to quit had surprised him so much: it was very out of character for him.

"Does Tristan's flirting bother you that much?" Jared asked, keeping his voice neutral. Talking about these things with his straight friends was always somewhat awkward. "If that's the problem, I'll tell him to cut it out."

Zach remained silent.

"Zach?" Jared said.

"I want to fuck him."

When Jared said nothing, Zach's lips twisted. "Stop looking at me like I've grown a second head."

Jared cleared his throat. "I thought you were straight."

"I am," Zach said with a pinched look. "I just really want to screw the little shit."

Jared cleared his throat again. This wasn't a conversation he had ever expected to have with Zach about Gabe's brother. "Aren't Donna and you still in an open relationship?"

Zach nodded curtly.

"Then what is the problem?"

"What's the problem?" Zach chuckled harshly. "Are you serious?"

"Are you freaking out because you're attracted to a guy?"

"No." Zach ran a hand over his face. "Maybe a little. I don't even like the brat. He drives me crazy. Half of the time, I want to throw him over my knee and—" He snapped his mouth shut and gave Jared a rueful smile. "It makes no sense. I've seen and touched hundreds of naked men, and okay, maybe none of them had such a pretty mouth—" Zach cut himself off again with a grimace. "It makes no bloody sense."

Jared couldn't really say he could relate. Women did nothing for him, no matter how beautiful they were.

"Talking to Gabriel would probably be more helpful for you than talking to me, though maybe not."

"Why not? I've always thought Gabriel was straight, too."

Jared looked at the picture on his desk.

It was a team photo, taken two years ago after winning the BPL trophy. Gabriel was leaning into him, his cheek pressed against Jared's, like a kitten starved for affection.

"It was different for Gabe," Jared said, tearing his eyes away from Gabriel's smiling lips. "He has always loved and needed me, so when we actually got together, sex was just a next step. Other men do nothing for him. He wants me because he loves me, rather than the other way around. He wouldn't know a thing about wanting a man he dislikes." He gave Zach a probing look. "You sure you can't control it? Do you really have to quit?"

A self-deprecating smile touched Zach's lips. "A few weeks ago, I gave him a spanking just because he went looking for sex after I had forbidden him, so I think it's pretty safe to say my professional judgment is compromised. Stop looking at me like that. I know: I shouldn't have done it. I know that. I just can't think clearly around the little shit." Zach raked his hand through his hair, frustration plain on his face. "When he's around, it's like my brain is located in my prick. I *have* to quit."

Jared studied him for a moment.

"Marriage is a very serious commitment. You must be completely committed to your relationship. Isn't it better to get this thing out of your system before the wedding and get on with your life?"

He received a withering look from Zach. "I really don't need this advice, Jared."

"Don't shoot the messenger," Jared said. "You know I'm right. You're still in an open relationship. Get it out of your system before marrying Donna. That would be the best for everyone involved."

Zach looked out of the window. "You're terrible at giving advice," he said. "You should have told me to keep my hands off him. Now I have a perfectly legitimate reason to do what I want."

"Is that such a bad thing?"

A harsh laugh left Zach's throat. He stood and grabbed his jacket. "I'll let you know soon."

Jared's frown deepened. Despite the advice he'd given Zach, the situation made him vaguely uneasy. Tristan was of age and more than capable of giving his consent, but…The situation was a mess. The fact that Tristan was Zach's patient wouldn't have been much of an issue—he would be a hypocrite to think that—except the nature of Zach's interest in Tristan was different from Jared's relationship with Gabe. Zach didn't love Tristan—he didn't even seem to like him. Zach just wanted Tristan and seemed to resent him a great deal for that.

"I know his groin is much better now, but keep in mind he's still injured," Jared said. *Translation: no angry, rough sex with one of my injured players.* "If you do it, be gentle." A part of him couldn't believe he was really having this conversation with one of his physiotherapists, but it had to be said. Tristan's health came first and foremost.

Zach smiled, as if Jared had said something very funny, and left.

Jared was left looking at the door in mild puzzlement as it closed after Zach.

He was still looking at the door when it opened again and Gabriel sauntered into the room.

"Lock the door," Jared said immediately.

Grinning and rolling his eyes, Gabriel did as he was told. "It's not like we ever have sex here."

"It doesn't stop you from molesting me here," Jared said with a look.

"Shut up, you love it." Gabe straddled Jared's lap and mouthed Jared's cheek. "Mmm. Why do you always smell so good?"

"You smell better," Jared said, pressing his nose into Gabriel's cheek and breathing him in. Christ. Sometimes he thought it wasn't possible to be so happy and so in love. He loved this boy. Loved him more than anything in the world.

His thoughts returned to Zach. He couldn't imagine being in Zach's position. Before he and Gabriel had become lovers, Jared had slept with other men, of course, but his attraction to them wasn't even a fraction of what he felt for Gabe, no matter how handsome those men were. It made him wonder about the strength of Zach's feelings for Donna. Was it really love if one was capable of wanting someone else so much?

But then again, it wasn't his place to judge. He and Gabriel weren't exactly the most normal couple in the world.

Gabe ran his fingers through Jared's hair. "I saw Zach. Is he finally sick of Tristan and wants to quit?"

Jared wondered how he was supposed to answer that. "Sort of."

"Sort of?" Gabriel pulled back and studied him curiously.

"Don't look at me like that. It's not my secret to tell."

"Jay."

"No."

"Jay."

Laughing, Jared kissed him again and again, until Gabe melted into him, forgetting all about Zach and his brother.

Chapter 12

Sitting in his car, Zach stared at the house. There was light downstairs, but otherwise the house was dark and quiet. It still surprised him a little how ordinary the house was. Even his own house was bigger and flashier than Tristan's. If he hadn't known better, he would have never guessed it was a famous football player's home. Maybe that was the point, because the security measures were non-existent. But then again, if the house had better security, he wouldn't be able to watch it for half an hour like some creepy stalker.

Zach shook his head with a grimace. Enough.

He got out of the car and walked toward the house as drops of rain started falling from the sky.

Zach refused to hesitate before knocking. He'd been acting ridiculously for weeks. Enough was enough.

The door opened and he tensed, but it was just Lydia. "Hey."

She blinked, looking at him in surprise. "Hey. Tristan said you quit."

Zach shook his head. "Is he home?"

She gestured upstairs. "Yeah, but I don't think it's a good idea to talk to him tonight. He's in a terrible mood." Lydia made a face and stepped aside, letting him in. "Been the entire day, actually. I had to cancel a very important press event. His PR manager is mad at me. Me, not Tristan! How is that my fault he's being a diva?"

"Has he trained today?"

"Yeah." She smiled crookedly. "But I think it was mostly to spite you and prove that he can do better without you. What did you do to piss him off so much? Made him eat too much healthy food?"

Zach averted his eyes. "I need to talk to him."

She gave him a sympathetic look. "Good luck with that. Lock the door after me."

"You're leaving?"

She opened the door. "I was on my way out. I've been here all day and it's ten already. I so need a break from him. I'm sure he can survive until morning without having someone at his beck and call. See you!"

Zach locked the door after Lydia, a furrow appearing between his brows. Her words made him wonder. He had a large, boisterous family, and although all of his siblings had moved out a while ago, they still spent a great deal of time at his house. But every time he'd seen Tristan, he was always alone. No friends or relatives ever seemed to visit him, despite his injury. Did he even have anyone?

Shaking the thought off, Zach headed upstairs. He wasn't here to understand the brat or feel sorry for him.

You shouldn't be here at all.

Zach took the steps slowly, his hand on the polished wooden banister, slow step after slow step. He felt a dryness in his mouth, his heart racing.

The small voice in the back of his mind kept telling him that he was making a mistake. He *wasn't* making a mistake. Jared was right: this needed to be done.

But no matter what he told himself, he couldn't shake off the feeling that he was doing something wrong.

He wasn't doing anything wrong. Donna wouldn't care. He and Donna had been in an off-and-on relationship for almost ten years and had been friends for twenty. Because of their jobs they often didn't see each other for months, so an open relationship was only practical for them, and both of them were fine with the other's getting laid while they were apart.

He had slept with dozens of other women over the course of their relationship and Donna had never been shy about her conquests, either. They joked and shared a laugh about it. In many ways, he and Donna were an old married couple, friends rather than passionate lovers.

Truth be told, they had never been particularly passionate, not even in their early twenties. Zach had never considered himself a passionate man. He had a healthy sex drive, but that was it. He was a rational man, always had been. His blood never went hot if he didn't allow it.

Never before had he met someone and just felt the overwhelming urge to shut them up—with his cock. This wasn't something that ever happened to him—until Tristan. This burning desire to have, take, fuck someone into the mattress was completely foreign. It was crude and base; it wasn't something he could explain or rationalize. He didn't want to make love or even have sex with Tristan—he wanted to fuck. It didn't seem to matter that Tristan was a guy, and that Zach didn't want guys. He wanted to screw that one.

There was nothing pretty about it.

It was as primitive as it got. It made him vaguely ashamed and disgusted, and a little incredulous that it was happening to him. His brothers would laugh their asses off if they found out that their eldest, responsible brother was acting on his instincts and drooling over a spoiled celebrity nine years his junior. Hell, Donna would laugh her ass off if she knew.

And yet, here he was. Because Jared was right: he had to get this thing out of his system before the wedding. The sooner he got rid of it, the better.

Zach pushed the door to Tristan's bedroom open.

The room was empty, but he could hear the water running in the en-suite bathroom. Tristan probably didn't even know there was someone else in the house.

He found his feet moving without his brain telling them to do so.

The bathroom was choked with shower steam. It was big and spacious, the shower large enough for five people, let alone one medium-sized guy. A very naked guy, who stood with his back to Zach, steam billowing up around him.

Zach had been a personal trainer or physiotherapist of many actors and sportsmen. For most of them, their bodies were the primary source of income; many of them were fit and good-looking, and some of them were flawlessly beautiful. But their bodies were Zach's job, nothing more.

Yet as his gaze followed the droplets of water running down the graceful curve of Tristan's back—his flawless golden skin—to the dimples above the swell of his perfectly rounded ass, Zach had to remind himself to breathe.

He was hard as a rock, his hands and mouth practically itching to touch and taste.

He wanted to bite and kiss that perfect little ass, bury his face against it and eat Tristan out, as he had wanted to do yesterday when Tristan was lying over his knee, his cheeks red from Zach's hands and so damn pretty that it had taken all his willpower not to spread the boy open and lick him until he was loose and ready for his cock. After Tristan had fallen asleep, it took only a few tugs of his cock to come like a schoolboy all over his hand.

He wasn't in any better state now.

His mouth dry, he watched as Tristan carefully soaped between his cheeks, his slim finger moving up and down before pushing inside. A small moan left Tristan's lips. Zach went still, realizing that Tristan was getting off rather than cleaning himself. His eyes zeroed in on that finger as Tristan widened his stance slightly and leaned his forehead against the shower wall to give himself better access. Jesus, the curve of his ass was downright obscene. Tristan's finger moved in and out of his hole, and Zach couldn't help but imagine the red tip of his cock disappearing inside it slowly. Shit.

Tristan pushed a second finger in and started finger-fucking himself with little gasps of pleasure that went straight to Zach's cock. Zach closed his eyes, trying to make himself leave. He should wait for Tristan in the bedroom. They needed to *talk*.

He had no delusions that he could leave the house without putting his prick inside the brat, but they needed to talk first. He had to make sure Tristan was on the same page and understood that sex would mean and change nothing.

Move, he told himself.

Zach moved—but not to leave the bathroom.

He moved toward Tristan, the water masking his approach.

He dropped to his knees on the bathroom tiles and, grabbing Tristan's hips, dragged his mouth across the smooth cheek.

Tristan's body went rigid, his fingers pulling out immediately. He attempted to turn around, but Zach was holding him still and Tristan could turn only his head. His face was flushed, his blue-green eyes wide, long dark lashes wet and glistening with water. He was so fucking pretty Zach's balls started aching as those soft, red lips formed a perfect "o." Tristan kept opening and closing his mouth wordlessly. Christ, he looked good enough to eat.

"What—" Tristan said, but his words turned into a moan as Zach gave his hole a long lick.

Spreading the cheeks open, Zach delved in, tasting clean skin and fruit-flavored lube. He'd never minded rimming women who asked him, but this was the first time he actually got off on doing it. Tristan's small, broken moans were such a huge turn on and Zach couldn't get enough. His body felt on fire, his cock throbbing with the urge to fuck. He couldn't wait anymore. Jesus, he needed to fuck him. It felt like he would die if he didn't put his cock in him.

Standing up, Zach shrugged off his drenched jacket, unzipped his jeans and pulled his aching cock out. "Lube," he said, pushing his fully clothed wet body against Tristan's naked one.

His fingers unsteady, Tristan reached out to the shelf and handed him the bottle of lube. Zach quickly smeared Tristan's hole with lube, pushed two fingers in and started scissoring them roughly. He was in no state to wait a second longer.

Sinking his teeth into Tristan's neck and sucking, he lubed up his cock and tried to line it up. The cock head nudged against Tristan's hole and they both grunted, but the angle was too awkward because of their height difference.

"You're too damn short," he said, hissing as his cock kept rubbing against Tristan's opening.

"I'm not," Tristan said, as contrary as ever.

Zach cursed and pulled away.

"Come on," he said, grabbing Tristan's arm and dragging him out of the bathroom. Along the way, he pulled his wet t-shirt off and kicked off his boots, but that was the extent of his patience.

The moment Tristan was on the bed, Zach was on top of him, his tongue in Tristan's mouth and cock grinding against his thigh.

It wasn't a gentle kiss or a sweet exploration. It was furious and raw, full of pent-up frustration and relief. He attacked Tristan's mouth with his lips and teeth, nipping and sucking as Tristan writhed underneath him. Christ, he wanted to consume the little shit, wanted to fuck him out of his system, out of his life. Tristan's tongue slipped into his mouth and his hands clung to Zach's hair, small gasps of pleasure slipping from his lips.

"Fuck," Tristan grunted. "Let's fuck. Please, please, let's fuck."

Zach stopped kissing him and took in a shuddering breath, trying to suppress the violent urge to throw the boy's legs over his shoulders and slam into him. He couldn't do it. He had to be careful. He must be careful. Tristan wasn't completely recovered yet.

He rolled off Tristan and pushed him onto his side.

"What are you—?"

"This way you're less likely to re-injure your groin," Zach said, spooning behind him and burying his face in Tristan's nape. "Lift your upper knee. Carefully. Don't move too abruptly. Don't strain your short adductors unnecessarily."

"I can't believe you," Tristan said with a groan. "This is not sexy at all."

With a harsh chuckle, Zach pressed his lips to the red mark he'd left on Tristan's neck yesterday and sucked. "This is not meant to be sexy." Taking his dripping cock into his hand, he pushed inside Tristan slowly.

He hissed as incredible tightness enveloped his cock. Jesus. When he bottomed out, Zach forced himself to be still. He hadn't prepped Tristan all that well. He had to give him time to adjust.

Tristan's breathing was coming in short gasps. "You're clean, right?"

Zach closed his eyes, grimacing. He couldn't believe he was so irresponsible. He was never irresponsible. "Yeah. You?"

"Sure." Tristan's body started relaxing around him. "Jared gets all of us checked for STDs every few weeks."

Something tightened in his gut. Zach sank his teeth into the vulnerable curve of Tristan's neck and slowly pulled out. "Jared said you flirted with him. Do you fancy him?"

Tristan laughed breathlessly. "He's the hottest man I've even seen. Of course I fancy him."

Zach slammed back in.

Gasping, Tristan turned his head and grinned at him dazedly. "Sorry, did I upset you?"

"Why would that upset me?"

He wrapped his arm around Tristan's waist and tugged him closer before starting to move in and out. It felt good but incredibly frustrating. The position didn't allow him a great range of movement and he couldn't fuck the brat as hard as he wanted—which was a good thing, considering Tristan's injury.

"Just saying," Tristan said cheekily. "You look a little green."

"You should be spanked every day," Zach gritted out, gripping Tristan's hip hard and thrusting into him slowly. Christ, he wanted to shove the boy under him and pound him into the mattress. This felt like a slow torture. "I couldn't care less who you fancy. Let's not pretend it's something it isn't. We just need to scratch the itch. That's it."

"Aw, you know how to make the guy feel special."

"It's not special," Zach said, covering Tristan's neck in wet, open-mouthed kisses. "It means nothing. We don't even like each other. It's just a fuck."

"True," Tristan said with a nice smile. "This is the worst fuck I've ever had."

"Is it?" Zach said in a low-pitched voice.

"Yup. So boring." Tristan yawned. "Wake me up when you're done—"

Zach shoved him onto his belly, making Tristan yelp. Screw it.

He pushed Tristan on his fours and slammed back inside him. Tristan moaned and fell onto his elbows, pushing back on Zach's cock.

Hissing, Zach finally started fucking him like he wanted to, his neck straining as he thrust into Tristan with abandon, fast and hard.

In all the times he had ever allowed himself to imagine being inside Tristan, he had never thought he would be so desperate or so out of control. But that was exactly how he was: desperate, out of control, arching and grinding and trying to crawl all the way up into the boy. Every thrust was harder and deeper, but he couldn't fuck Tristan hard enough as he drank in the sight of him: his beautiful back and ass, and his own cock pistoning in and out of Tristan's hole. Tristan was making low, shameless noises, moving back to meet his thrusts, as if he couldn't get enough of his cock.

"You were saying?" Zach ground out, grunting with every thrust.

"Fuck you—oh god—more."

Zach gave him more, until the world blurred into watercolors around him, faster and faster—so perfect, so good—and then he could feel Tristan coming, clenching down, shaking, and Zach kept pounding him right through it because he couldn't stop either; he was so close. Finally, when Tristan's legs just seemed to give out, making Tristan fall face first onto the bed, Zach went down with him, groaning and pushing deep. Then he was coming so hard his vision whited out. It felt like he was coming forever, pumping himself into Tristan until he couldn't anymore. His arms gave out and he closed his eyes, completely spent and sated.

He should probably move. Women always complained that he was too heavy. But Tristan didn't say anything, so he didn't move, mouthing the sweaty skin of Tristan's neck. His cock was still nestled inside the boy and he had little desire to pull it out.

Silence felt good. His body was completely sated, the maddening pent-up frustration finally gone.

He knew Tristan wasn't asleep—he kept squirming a little against Zach's lips but remained quiet.

"Sex is such a silly thing," Tristan murmured suddenly, his voice muffled. "Don't you think?"

"Hmm?" Zach said, dragging his lips across Tristan's neck. He'd never before thought necks could be beautiful. Tristan's was.

"Sex makes people behave stupidly and gives an illusion of intimacy." Tristan's tone was thoughtful, almost wistful. "It's so stupid."

Zach frowned, his blissed-out brain wanting nothing more than to sleep. Then he realized he was still kissing the brat's neck. He stopped. Clearing his throat, he searched for something to say. "It's normal," he said, in his driest voice. "Orgasm generally produces a spike in oxytocin's levels and leads to feelings of closeness, intimacy—"

"Stop. Just stop. I can't believe you're still lecturing me when you have your prick in me." Tristan yawned. "Night."

And just like that, he was asleep.

Now it was definitely time to leave.

Zach didn't move. He would.

In a little while.

Chapter 13

Tristan awoke to the sounds of birds chirping outside his bedroom window. He was sprawled half on top of something big and warm, and something soft was tickling his nose. He opened his eyes blearily and blinked a few times before everything sharpened into focus.

Oh.

He was snuggled up into Zach's side, his arm and leg slung over the other man's body and his face pressed into Zach's armpit. He inhaled carefully. It should have been gross. It wasn't. The warm, male, musky scent made him a little dizzy—in a good way. He inhaled again, relishing how good his body felt. Well-rested, well-fucked, and comfy.

Tristan looked at Zach, who was still dead to the world. The early sunlight brought out the little golden highlights in his rich brown hair. Tristan stared in fascination. He'd never seen hair like Zach's before: it seemed brown most of the time, but in certain light his hair could take on a bit of a reddish or golden hue.

Then his sleep-addled brain registered something far more important: they had spent the night together.

At some point during the night, Zach must have undressed fully: he was as naked as Tristan was.

Tristan worried his lip. This was all so very strange to him. He had never woken up with a man in his bed—he'd never actually brought a man home; it would be suicidal for his career. It had always been anonymous sex with faceless strangers in dark clubs.

He had never been willing to risk his career for a fuck. He wasn't like Gabriel, who was stupid enough not to care about consequences if people found out about his relationship with Jared. The funniest thing was, Gabriel wasn't even gay; Tristan was pretty sure Jared was the only man Gabe had ever been attracted to. It was pretty ironic that his mostly straight adoptive brother was completely unashamed of his relationship with another man, while he, Tristan, couldn't be gayer and yet he was so scared of being outed that he didn't let any of his male lovers get a good look at his face.

Maybe some would call him a coward. Maybe he *was* a coward, but it was practical. He had worked so hard to get where he was now; it would be foolish to lose it over sex. Shagging women may not be satisfying or arousing—it felt like a chore at best if he managed to get it up at all—but he was forced to do it for appearances' sake once in a while, and he had never brought those women home.

So all in all, this was his first time sleeping with someone.

Tristan's eyes traveled down Zach's body. He licked his lips. He had lied when he told Zach that Jared was the hottest man he had ever seen. Jared was classically handsome, his looks making most Hollywood actors pale in comparison, but Tristan never felt dizzy with desire to have Jared naked and on top of him.

"I didn't take you for a cuddler."

Tristan's gaze snapped to Zach's face, a wave of embarrassment sweeping over him as he met all-too-alert gray eyes. He suddenly became very aware of his arm and leg slung over Zach's body and the fact that his head was nestled in Zach's armpit. Tristan didn't move away; if he did, it would prove that there was something wrong with his behavior in the first place. He wasn't responsible for his behavior while he slept.

Inhaling carefully, Tristan tried to think of something scathing to say and couldn't.

He had no clue how to behave in this situation. This was his first morning after.

Tristan decided he didn't like mornings after. He definitely didn't like how vulnerable and unsure he felt. Zach's eyes always seemed to see right through him and right now Tristan felt like an open book.

"I'm not a cuddler," he said with a scowl. "I was just cold."

Zach just looked at him for a moment but didn't comment. "How is your groin?" he asked instead.

Groaning, Tristan rolled his eyes. "Really?"

"Yes. This is my job." Zach untangled himself from Tristan's limbs and sat up. His fingers started prodding and kneading Tristan's groin muscles experimentally. "Any pain?"

Gazing at the ceiling, Tristan wondered what Zach would do if he complained that there was an ache in his cock.

"No."

"Looks good," Zach concluded finally.

"It *is* good. I told you—I'm ready to begin real training. My groin doesn't bother me anymore."

"Absence of pain during normal daily activities can be deceiving. It's different from the forces involved in training or competition. But it looks good. We'll increase the intensity and frequency of training."

Tristan looked at him. "Really?"

"Really. You're ready to start jogging."

Tristan eyed him in bewilderment. It was all very normal, as if they hadn't had sex and weren't naked in bed together. "Why are you…?"

Zach raised his eyebrows. "Why am I what?"

"Why aren't you having a gay freak-out?" Tristan asked. "Why aren't you feeling guilty or angry—or something? Why are you so calm?"

"What is the point?" Zach said in the same calm, rational tone. "What's done is done. I'm not proud of it or anything, but it needed to be done. Now that we've finally dealt with it, we can move on and get on with our lives—and your training."

He got off the bed, presenting Tristan with a magnificent view of his wide, strong back and firm buttocks. "It's done and over. There's no point being angry over nothing now. You're my patient. I'm your physiotherapist. Now get your bottom out of bed. We're behind schedule as it is."

Tristan stared at his back, his confusion slowly being replaced by another, darker emotion. He felt like laughing and throwing something at Zach's head at the same time. So Zach was casting him aside like a used condom, eager to forget and move on. Great. Fine. *Fine.* That was what Tristan wanted, too: no strings attached was his life motto. Fine.

When Tristan didn't say anything, Zach turned around and looked at Tristan.

Tristan could well imagine what he looked like. His lips were sore, swollen from the bruising kisses. He had stubble rash all over his cheeks and chin. His hair was messier than ever as he ran his fingers through it. He knew his neck was covered in hickeys. There were finger-shaped bruises on his hips. In short, he felt well-fucked and he probably looked it.

Zach averted his eyes and reached for his clothes, his movements jerky. "Stop looking at me like that and get out of the bed."

"Like what?" Tristan said, cocking his head and looking at Zach from under his eyelashes.

"Like a slut needing a cock."

Tristan refused to take the bait and become angry. His heavily-lidded eyes skimmed down Zach's chest to his taut stomach, and then lower, to his thick erection. Wetting his lips, he returned his gaze to Zach's face and spread his legs. He didn't need to say anything. His eyes said everything for him. *Come here. Fuck me. You know you want to.*

Before Tristan knew it, Zach was on him, pinning him down with his heavy body. "You—" he bit out before kissing Tristan, again and again. God. Tristan curled one hand around Zach's neck and reached down between them to grab Zach's cock. "In," he mumbled, trying to guide it inside him. "Get in."

"Lube," Zach said, sucking on his lips. It was kind of hilarious that they both were reduced to monosyllabic words so quickly.

"Don't care." Tristan gasped as the cock head nudged his hole. He was still a little slick after last night—the lube was long-lasting and difficult to clean up. "Fuck me."

"Don't be silly," Zach managed, but his hips were

already moving, his cock grinding into him until the head finally slipped inside. Tristan panted, his glazed eyes wide and fingers digging into Zach's back. God, Zach's cock in him felt amazing, so bloody perfect, the girth stretching him to his limits, pleasure mixing with pain, and pain becoming pleasure.

With a groan, Zach dropped his head beside Tristan's on the pillow, and started fucking him with hard, urgent thrusts. Squirming, Tristan wrapped his legs around Zach's waist, whimpers coming out of his mouth every time the cock in him hit his prostate. It wasn't sex; it was *necessity*, something they both craved and needed. It was dirty, fast and shameless, a clash of bodies, teeth and lips, and want, so much want, it made him dizzy, giddy, and shameless. His senses were overstimulated to the point that he had the irrational thought that he might die if Zach pulled out of him. Zach thrust, hard, over and over, and Tristan held on, muttering something unintelligible and reveling in the breathing and the hot, perfect thrusts and Zach's grunts and knowing that yes, fuck yes, this was what they both needed.

His orgasm was frightening in its intensity and Tristan pulled Zach closer as he came, clenching hard around Zach's cock. The spasms were so powerful he would have shaken his way right off the bed if Zach hadn't been pinning him down. Zach slammed into him a few more times and went still on top of him, boneless and heavy and so damn perfect. Tristan whimpered in pleasure, tightening his arms around him.

The hush in the room was deafening.

Unlike their first time, this time neither of them fell asleep.

They both were wide awake.

Tristan stared at the ceiling over Zach's bare shoulder and wondered how he was supposed to act. His legs were still wrapped around Zach's hips. Tristan thought, not without humor, that at least now they knew for sure his groin was definitely more than fine for more vigorous exercises: he didn't feel any discomfort.

Zach sighed and then his mouth pressed against the side of Tristan's neck. A soft kiss. Another one. And another.

Tristan smirked. He had heard that sex turned some men soft and affectionate afterward. He'd never thought Zach would be one of them—he didn't seem the type—but apparently Zach was. Tristan idly pondered whether he should comment on it and embarrass Zach. The soft kisses and touches didn't feel horrible, but he couldn't waste such a golden opportunity to make fun of Zach, could he?

"Who knew sex could turn you into such a softie," he said with a snort.

The kisses stopped.

Tristan pursed his lips.

"That's pretty rich coming from a guy who's hugging me like I'm his teddy bear," Zach murmured.

Flushing, Tristan untangled his arms and legs from around Zach and scowled. "Get off me. You weigh a ton." As soon as Zach rolled off him, Tristan got out of the bed and headed to the bathroom. "Use the bathroom down the hall," he threw over his shoulder. "You stink."

"You always must have the last word, huh?"

Tristan opened the bathroom door, looked back at Zach, who was sitting on the bed with a dark look on his face. Tristan smiled and blew him a kiss. "Always."

Zach stared at him oddly and Tristan quickly shut the door and cringed. Sex must have addled his brain, too.

Chapter 14

Two weeks later

"Hey," Zach said, closing and locking the front door.

Lydia looked up from the pile of letters in her lap and smiled. "Hey." She looked uncertainly at the keys in Zach's hand.

"I asked for a spare key after the little prince overslept for the third time and couldn't be bothered to get out of bed to open the door," Zach explained, putting his keys back into his pocket.

Lydia snorted. "That's pretty much how I got a spare key." She looked at Zach curiously. "But I thought you'd already come and gone today. I thought the training session was in the morning."

Shrugging, Zach walked over. "I thought it was your day off."

Lydia shot him a sharp look but didn't comment on the change of subject. "I'm a little behind on fan mail. I have to finish going through these and give the non-creepy ones to Tristan to respond."

That gave Zach pause. "He actually does it himself?"

She smiled. "I know, right? Doesn't sound like him, but I guess it strokes his ego to read all the gushing letters."

"Hmm." Zach picked up one of the letters. Skimming through it, he shook his head. Sometimes he forgot how famous Tristan was.

"Zach?"

He looked up and found Lydia chewing on her lip.

"Can I ask you something?" she said.

"Sure."

Lydia hesitated before saying slowly, "Tristan has been strange lately."

After a moment, Zach asked, "Strange?"

"He's...distracted and—just weird. For example, I was late by four minutes yesterday and he didn't even say anything!"

"It's just four minutes, Lydia," Zach said, looking back at the letter. "Not the end of the world."

"Come on, you know him! He's constantly bored and gets a kick out of threatening to fire me for the silliest reasons. But this time he didn't bitch at all!"

Zach laughed. "Shouldn't you be glad he didn't?"

"I—of course I am. It's just strange."

"Not that strange," he said.

"But that's not all. I think he's seeing someone."

Slowly, Zach looked up from the letter. "Seeing someone?"

Lydia nodded. "Haven't you seen his neck? The love bites? He used to scoff when he saw someone's love bites and now he's..."

"Tristan is fit enough to have sex," Zach said, putting the letter down. "That's the only thing I care about." He glanced upstairs. "Is he home? I need to talk to him."

"He is," she said, returning her attention to the fan mail.

Zach headed upstairs, relieved that he didn't have to answer more of her questions. He'd never been comfortable lying. He liked Lydia and lying to her didn't sit well with him. Of course, technically he hadn't lied to her. Tristan wasn't seeing anyone. They just had sex. Sometimes.

Zach nearly laughed out loud.

Sometimes?

More like every day. Sometimes twice a day. The worst part was, they couldn't keep it strictly to the bedroom. Like yesterday, in the middle of an argument Tristan grabbed his head and pulled him in for a hungry, bruising kiss and Zach's prick somehow ended up in Tristan's mouth.

In the past two weeks, those little incidents had been happening with a disturbing, ever-increasing frequency and intensity.

That was why he had to end it. Their no-strings-attached arrangement was bleeding into their professional relationship. No matter what he told himself, it *wasn't* okay to start kissing Tristan's thighs during a sports massage. It wasn't. His lack of professionalism when it came to Tristan was grating. It couldn't go on like that. At least he had already taken steps to put an end to this. For starters, he had managed not to touch Tristan this day.

The day isn't over yet, his inner voice said snidely. His inner voice sounded disturbingly like Tristan lately.

Zach ignored it. He wasn't here for that. He hadn't lied to Lydia: he really needed to talk to Tristan. Jared had called him and asked about Tristan's progress.

Apparently the club higher-ups wanted Tristan back on the pitch.

Although Jared didn't let them bully him, he asked Zach to accelerate Tristan's rehabilitation program if Tristan was ready. That was why Zach was here: to talk. And nothing else.

Tristan was in his bedroom, seated on the couch with a tablet in his hands. He didn't look up when Zach entered.

Closing the door, Zach said, "Jared wants me to accelerate your rehabilitation program."

"About time," Tristan said, his eyes still on his tablet. "And you couldn't have called to tell me that?"

Zach opened his mouth and closed it.

"Go away," Tristan said. "I hate it when people stare at me."

Zach studied him. Tristan seemed...angry. "Lydia thinks you're seeing someone."

Tristan snorted without looking up from his tablet.

Zach walked over and crossed his arms over his chest. "Look at me when I'm talking to you."

"Why?"

Because when I'm in the room, you should always look at me. Zach had to bite his tongue to stop himself from saying that. What the hell?

"Look at me," Zach said again.

Tristan lifted his blue-green eyes, and a rush of want hit Zach so hard and fast his breath caught in his throat. If he believed in such things, he would have thought the boy was an incubus, because there was nothing rational about this heady want and this desire to kiss that scowling pretty mouth and *have*. He didn't understand it, couldn't explain it or rationalize it. This was ridiculous. It wasn't him. He wasn't this man. He wouldn't be this man.

"Stop telling me what to do," Tristan said sullenly. "And I thought we were done for today?"

"We are."

Tristan arched an eyebrow, all haughty arrogance. "Leave, then. Don't you see I'm busy? I don't have time for you."

No one could get under his skin like Tristan.

Putting a hand on the back of the couch, Zach leaned down so they were face to face. "What's gotten into you, brat?" he said, his voice softer than he had intended.

Tristan swallowed before glaring. "Nothing. I just don't like that you assume that you're the one calling the shots. I'm not in the mood for you. If you think you can come here whenever you want and stick your prick in me, think again." His full lips pursed, the bottom one poking out.

"I'm not here for sex," Zach said, dragging his eyes away from that mouth. "I told you yesterday that was the last time."

Humor flashed across Tristan's face and vanished. "Just like you told me the day before yesterday? And the day before that?"

Zach's jaw clenched. "This time I mean it. I haven't touched you today, have I?"

Tristan gave him a vicious glare.

Zach went still as something occurred to him. "You wanted me to touch you." That wasn't a question.

Putting his hands on Zach's chest, Tristan tried to shove him away. "I told you to get out."

Zach didn't budge. His hand found itself on Tristan's cheek. "You wanted me to kiss you?" His voice dropped to a rough rasp as he leaned in. Maybe one more kiss. Just one. A very short one. And then they were done.

"No," Tristan said, his hands moving up Zach's chest.

"You're usually a better liar than this," Zach murmured before molding their mouths together. They both moaned, hands burying in each other's hair as they kissed deeply. Had it been just a day? Too damn long.

"Tristan, I finished the—"

They sprang apart, breathing hard.

Lydia stood in the doorway, her eyes wide and dozens of letters at her feet.

"Oh," she said weakly.

"If you tell someone," Tristan said tightly. "I'll make sure you'll never find another job."

Lydia paled.

Sighing, Zach pinched the bridge of his nose. "Lydia, please wait for me downstairs." She practically ran out of the room and Zach turned to Tristan. "Blackmail isn't how normal people deal with every situation."

Tristan sprang to his feet. "But I have to talk to her and make sure she—"

Zach grabbed him and turned him around. "You aren't going anywhere. You will not threaten her."

Tristan just stared at him wide-eyed, shaking his head over and over. He was hyperventilating.

"Calm down," Zach said firmly but not without kindness, squeezing Tristan's shoulders. "Nothing will happen. She won't tell anyone. I'll deal with it. I promise."

Tristan's breathing evened out a little, and the tremors stopped, but those eyes…Goddammit.

Zach leaned in and brushed his lips against Tristan's.

They both went still.

Tristan exhaled shakily.

Zach pulled back and walked out of the room. He ran his hand through his hair as he took the stairs down. He was going mad. Crazy. Bloody insane.

Lydia stood in the middle of the living room, her arms crossed over her chest. Her face was grim, her brown eyes full of judgment.

Zach sighed, tired of the conversation before it even started. "It isn't what it looks like."

"Wow, really? I know what I saw." She shook her head, looking incredulous. "I can't—can't believe you. I thought you could see what a horrible little monster he is."

Tristan's panic-stricken, vulnerable expression flashed through his mind. Zach pushed it away, irrationally wishing he had never seen it. He had seen Tristan vulnerable before, of course—Tristan always looked soft and vulnerable (and *beautiful*) after Zach spanked him (which was why Zach tried not to do it too often, no matter how much they both enjoyed it)—but this was different. He could excuse the rush of protectiveness after he spanked Tristan as a side effect; *this* he couldn't excuse as easily.

"Look," Zach said. "What you saw is…it's complicated."

"No shit. What about Donna?"

"It has nothing to do with her. I'm not cheating on her. We have an open relationship, have had for ages. This is not hurting anyone."

Lydia's forehead wrinkled. "An open relationship? So close to the wedding?"

Zach gave a shrug. "We're adults. We often don't see each other for months because of our jobs. We have needs. An open relationship has always worked for us. Until the wedding we both can sleep with other people."

A puzzled expression appeared on Lydia's face. "I don't understand. If an open relationship works so well for you, why are you getting married and going exclusive?"

"For many reasons."

Zach thought back to his conversation with Donna half a year ago. There had been no grand proposal. Neither he nor Donna was the sentimental, romantic type. They both were rational people, who loved each other and had known for ages that they would end up getting married eventually.

They had simply sat down and discussed it. They agreed that it was the right time: they both had turned thirty that year, and it was probably time to settle down. Their families had been nagging them to tie the knot for years. Donna wanted kids. Zach wouldn't mind kids, either; truth be told, now that all his siblings had moved out, the house felt too big for one man. Besides, Donna was getting a promotion soon and a desk job, so all the stars were aligned. The timing was perfect.

There had never been a question that they would stop sleeping with other people after getting married. They both took marriage seriously—that was why they had been putting it off for so long.

Zach looked back at Lydia. "There are many reasons, but mostly, we believe in monogamy in marriage. This— this thing with Tristan isn't hurting anyone and isn't going to change anything."

"Are you sure of that?"

"Yes."

"All right. I'm sorry for jumping to conclusions, then." She was still frowning. "It's just...I can't believe you're jeopardizing your relationship for *him*."

"I'm not jeopardizing anything. If Donna asks, I'll tell her. I have nothing to hide. It's just sex and sex means nothing." If anything, Donna would probably find it funny and think he was having an early mid-life crisis.

"I didn't even know you swung that way."

"That's the thing: I don't." Zach rubbed his eyes tiredly. "He just pushes all the right—wrong—buttons on me."

She snorted. "He pushes all the wrong buttons on me too, but you don't see me sucking his lips." She shook her head. "I can't believe you can be attracted to such a piece of shit. He's actually threatening to ruin my career!" Her face turned red, her eyes flashing. "We'll see about it!"

Zach tensed. "Don't tell anyone he's gay. You know that would destroy his career."

She looked mutinous. "Good. That would serve him right!"

"You're not that spiteful, Lydia," Zach said calmly. "You're better than that. Forget about his threats. He was just scared and wanted to protect himself. He didn't mean it."

Lydia stared at him as if she was seeing him for the first time. "Oh my god." There was disappointment on her face. Disappointment, horror, and pity. "Honey, get away from him before it's too late." And with that, she left, her heels clicking loudly on the hardwood.

It took Zach a moment to register her meaning—what she was implying—and he almost laughed. He followed her out of the house.

"If you really think what I think you meant, you're being ridiculous," he said when he caught up with her.

"Oh yeah?" Lydia said, her voice dripping with sarcasm. "Before you know it, you'll be saying what a nice person he is. Please. God, *men*. Is he that good at sucking cock?"

"Don't be silly," Zach said. "He's definitely not the nicest person around. He's a total brat, but it's not a crime. I've met worse. I've had far worse clients than him. I don't know why you hate him so much."

"Why?" She stopped and turned to him. "Fine, I'll tell you why. From the very first day he hired me, he has treated me like a slave who is there for his amusement. I'm not a person to him. I'm a punching bag for his temper when he gets tired of pretending to be the Golden Boy. He takes out all his frustrations on me. He has a very cruel sense of humor and he never gives a damn that he might hurt my feelings. And the worst thing is, I always have to suck it up and say nothing, because I need this job! I'm not like you—I'm a nobody—and I can't quit just because I want to. I hate working for him, but I need the money, and I can't just quit because he's a rich prick who has everything so damn easy!"

She looked on the verge of tears. Angry tears. "And it makes me sick that most people have no clue what a malicious person he is. I thought you could see him for what he is—I thought you were like me—but now he has you fooled, too."

"No, he doesn't," Zach said. "And to be fair, I don't think he always had it easy. He's an orphan."

She scoffed. "Oh yeah, the 'poor orphan' card. Please. The public laps it up, but it's just a sob story to get people's sympathy."

Zach wondered why he hadn't noticed before the extent of Lydia's bitterness and animosity toward Tristan. Her quips had always seemed merely snarky and amusing.

"Yes, but it isn't necessarily a lie," he said.

"Honey, he's sucking your brain through your prick."

"He's doing no such thing," Zach said with a grimace.

"He is," she hissed. "You should know better. He's ugly, Zach. He's ugly on the inside, trust me on this. He has no redeemable qualities and everyone who really knows him knows that. Why do you think he has no real friends? No meaningful relationships, despite all his fame and looks? Even his own brother can't stand him! No one loves him as a person. He might look beautiful, but he's toxic, shallow, and fake. Behind his beautiful facade, there is no soul. Leave the job before he poisons your mind any further."

Zach bit the inside of his cheek. She was starting to irritate him, even though he'd had similar thoughts not a long time ago. "You're being melodramatic. I have everything under control."

"Yeah, I saw how you had everything under control when you had your tongue down his throat."

"Look," Zach said, his voice more clipped than he would have liked. "I appreciate your concern, but I have everything under control. I'm asking you to keep quiet about it. If not for his sake, then for mine. Please. I'd really appreciate it."

Lydia pursed her lips. "All right. But remember what I said. He's a toxic piece of shit and he's not worth the trouble—"

"I'll keep that in mind," Zach bit off and headed back to the house, uncurling his fingers and flexing them. He wasn't even sure why her words had rubbed him the wrong way. She wasn't entirely wrong.

And why hadn't he told her that he and Tristan were done? Because they were done.

"What did she say?" Tristan asked the moment he entered the house.

Narrowly avoiding colliding into him, Zach closed the door.

Tristan was worrying his lip, his eyes wary and anxious.

"She agreed not to tell anyone," Zach said.

"I don't trust her." A deep furrow appeared between Tristan's brows. "She hates me."

"If you were nicer to her, you would have had no reason to worry."

Tristan chuckled. "I have to be nice to everyone all the time. Do you know how exhausting it is? I pay her an obscene amount of money for the privilege not to be nice to her."

"Is that a clause in her contract?" Zach said, unimpressed.

Tristan frowned, looking like the thought had never occurred to him. "Well, no. Should it have been?"

Zach couldn't help but laugh. "You're unbelievable." He grabbed him by the shirt and dragged him into a kiss. The brat sighed and all but melted into him, his hands coming up to grab Zach's hair, his soft plush lips parting with eagerness that made Zach's cock throb. Jesus, that mouth. How could someone so poisonous have such a sweet mouth?

Zach growled when Tristan took his mouth away.

"Lube's upstairs," Tristan said, flushed and so damn pretty it hurt to look at him and not have him.

Tristan grabbed Zach's hand and dragged him upstairs.

And Zach let him. Of course he did. Son of a bitch, the boy really was sucking his brain through his cock.

But this is the last time, he vowed as he pushed Tristan into the bed.

Liar, Tristan's voice said in his head as Tristan's body sucked him in, tight, sweet, and scorching.

Chapter 15

"Slow down. You're running too fast. And remember what I told you about your running technique."

Tristan rolled his eyes, although Zach was behind him and couldn't see it. "I'm a professional sportsman. I'll have you know my running technique is perfect!"

"Your hips are behind your feet again," Zach said.

Looking back, Tristan caught Zach's eyes and smiled. "Maybe you should focus on my running technique and stop watching my hips." He turned away and continued jogging, wishing he could take it back. Sex-addled brain? Case in point. They were training, for God's sake. He wasn't supposed to bring it up—whatever this thing was—while they were jogging. Right now they were a patient and his physiotherapist, and what they sometimes did after the training sessions wasn't supposed to interfere with their professional relationship.

Of course their professional relationship had never been very professional to begin with, but after the Lydia fiasco last week, they had to be more careful. The silly bint was now always around, sticking her nose where it didn't belong.

She watched their training sessions in the gym with suspicious, wary eyes, as though she wanted to keep Zach out of Tristan's evil clutches. It was kind of hilarious at first, but it had quickly become annoying and frustrating.

Tristan would have fired her already, but Zach had convinced him otherwise. Zach was right: she was more likely to tell people about his sexuality if Tristan fired her. But it didn't mean Tristan was happy about her being around.

"Mind your hips, and your feet will take care of themselves," Zach said, his tone cool and very professional. Zach had been making a lot of effort to be professional around him. Whatever Lydia had told him clearly hit a nerve. Tristan wasn't stupid: it was obvious Zach wanted this thing between them to end. Obviously Tristan wanted the same thing. Obviously.

Now they just had to figure out how to stop.

"Foot strike is just the end result of other things happening farther up the kinetic chain," Zach said.

"Yeah, whatever," Tristan said, glancing around. The park was empty at such a ridiculously early hour. He stole a glance at Zach and chose the path that led into the woods.

"Tristan." The warning in Zach's voice was unmistakable.

Tristan ignored it and continued jogging, knowing that Zach would follow. He would be pissed off, but he would follow.

He always did.

Tristan veered off the path and came to a halt in a small clearing in the woods. Leaning his cheek against the trunk of a tree, Tristan closed his eyes, breathing in the fresh scent of dirt and spring.

"Tristan," Zach said, his voice tight and angry.

A firm body pressed against Tristan and the familiar lips dragged across his cheek, stubble scratching his sensitive skin.

Tristan shivered. "Don't you own a good razor?" he grumbled, leaning back into Zach's warmth. It was a chilly morning; that was all.

"Do you think you're subtle?" Zach said, his hand slipping under Tristan's hoodie and stroking his bare stomach.

No. I just need your lips and hands on me.

Tristan grimaced at his train of thought and said sulkily, "No one forced you to follow me here."

Zach laughed, as if he'd said something funny. "You knew I'd follow you." Zach nuzzled into Tristan's ear, the hand on his stomach slipping into Tristan's sweatpants and cupping his half-hard cock.

"Of course I'd follow you," Zach ground out, jerking him off with rough strokes. "You're a bloody siren."

"Sirens were female," Tristan said incoherently, his eyes sliding shut.

"Sirens were beautiful creatures who lured foolish men to their deaths."

Tristan grinned. "I'm flattered—" He groaned when Zach pulled his hand out.

Zach bit his earlobe and muttered hoarsely, "Wanna be in you, dollface. But not now. Not here."

A whine escaped Tristan's lips. Why not? It had been almost a day since they'd had sex.

"Don't call me that," he said belatedly, trying to pull himself together.

Zach took a deep breath and stepped back. "Let's go," he said briskly. "You have one more mile to run."

Tristan looked down at the erection tenting his sweatpants and glared at him. "Sadist."

Zach smirked.

He wanted to kiss that smirk off his face.

Tristan froze.

"What?" Zach said, frowning a little.

"Nothing." Tristan jogged away.

* * *

"Why do you live here?"

Tristan opened an eye and looked up at Zach. "Huh?" he murmured, still a little dazed after his orgasm. Zach's heart beat steadily under his cheek, no longer hammering.

"This is a good house," Zach said, his voice still a bit hoarse. "But it's not exactly the sort of house celebrities live in."

"You know I don't do pillow talk," Tristan said, closing his eyes again.

"Your head is on my chest, so technically, it's not pillow talk."

Tristan pinched Zach's side. "You're not funny."

Zach's fingers carded through his hair, his blunt nails scratching Tristan's scalp. God. So good.

Tristan sighed softly and mumbled, "But if you must know, I used to own a very fancy mansion. Bought it only because I could."

"Used to?"

"Sold it."

"Why?"

Tristan made a face. He'd bought the mansion for one reason: to have a fancier house than his father's and to rub it in his face. But it hadn't taken him long to realize how lame it was. Arthur Grayson wouldn't know and wouldn't care even if he did.

"It was just a good investment," Tristan said, opening his eyes. He smirked at Zach. "Sold it for twice the price to a Russian billionaire who was eager to buy a football star's house. Such a dumbass. I lived a week in that house."

Zach shook his head with a smile. "You're—"

"Very smart, I know," Tristan said, rubbing his cheek against Zach's chest and yawning.

Zach stared at him.

"What?" Tristan muttered with a sleepy smile.

Zach scrambled out of the bed and started getting dressed. "I have to go," he said roughly, zipping up his jeans.

Tristan blinked up at him. It wasn't as though Zach stayed every night—he stayed only when the sex lasted well into the night, when he was too spent to leave. Like tonight.

"It's two in the morning," Tristan said.

"Precisely," Zach said, slipping into his jacket.

And then he was gone.

Frowning, Tristan rolled over and buried his face in the pillow. It smelled of Zach. It was annoying. Tristan considered getting another pillow, but it seemed too much of an effort. This one would have to do.

He closed his eyes, breathed in, and let himself drift away.

Chapter 16

Two days later, Zach found himself alone with Lydia for the first time since she had walked in on them.

"You still sure you have everything under control?" Lydia said after Tristan disappeared upstairs to take a shower.

Zach looked at her and said, "Yes."

"Have you seen the way you look at him?"

He didn't even want to know.

"Let it go, Lydia," he said with a sigh, dropping himself onto the couch.

Lydia gave him a stubborn look he'd become very familiar with. "Why are you still here? It's afternoon."

Zach met her eyes steadily. "We had to accelerate Tristan's rehabilitation program. He has training sessions twice a day now."

She pursed her lips, clearly not believing him. "But—"

"Look, I didn't want to be rude, but it's none of your business," he said as gently as he could.

It wasn't particularly gentle. He liked Lydia, he did, but he was getting fed up with her constant interference.

He really wasn't in the mood for another rant about Tristan's evilness and how Zach should put an end to this.

He didn't need any reminding. He knew what he should do, had known all along. The execution was just a little elusive.

"Sorry," she said, awkwardly. "I know I can get a bit carried away. Okay, I'll go. It's not like I'm welcome here. I'm surprised he didn't kick me out already."

"I'm trying to keep him from firing you, but you aren't helping, you know."

She gave him an odd look. "He actually listens to you?"

Zach shrugged. "He's not as unreasonable as you think."

Silence.

He could see how badly she wanted to argue with him. At last, she sighed. "Okay, you know my opinion. I'm not gonna say it again." She grabbed her purse. "Tell him his PR manager said it would be good if he takes Darcy Peyton to some posh restaurant tonight to celebrate."

"Celebrate what?"

"His birthday," Lydia said, shutting the door after her.

It was Tristan's birthday?

Zach frowned. Tristan's routine hadn't changed at all. There were no phone calls, no friends or family members congratulating him, no gifts. Nothing. Tristan acted like it was an ordinary day.

After a few minutes, he heard bare feet padding downstairs and braced himself mentally.

"She left?" Tristan said, wiping his torso with a big, fluffy towel. He was wearing only a pair of shorts, riding low on his hips.

"Yeah," Zach said, dragging his eyes away. "She said your PR manager wants you to take Darcy Peyton to a restaurant tonight."

A look of confusion crossed Tristan's face. "Who's Darcy Peyton?"

Zach said neutrally, "Maybe your beard?"

Tristan's eyebrows knit for a beat, then his expression cleared. "Right. Probably." He pulled a face. "Not quite in the mood for vagina." He gave Zach a hungry once-over, licking those plump lips of his. "I'd rather have your cock."

The cock in question twitched in Zach's pants, springing to half-mast.

Zach grimaced, cursing inwardly but unsurprised. When he was around Tristan, he wasn't the one controlling his prick. Never mind that they'd already had sex that morning before Lydia's arrival. He hadn't intended to, but Tristan had looked flushed and
sleepy and soft, and Zach just hadn't been able to resist touching him. Pretty damn pathetic.

"I didn't know today is your birthday," Zach said harshly, trying to pull himself together. Giving in to his weakness once a day was bad enough. He could walk away without putting his prick into the boy one more time. He could.

"It's a day like any other," Tristan said, sauntering his way towards Zach. "Never understood why people make such a big fuss over it. I guess it's something to celebrate for parents, but my mother's dead, so..." He straddled Zach's thighs.

"What about your dad?"

Tristan's hand paused on Zach's zipper. A shadow crossed his face before he unzipped Zach's pants and shoved his hand inside.

Zach hissed as Tristan's slim fingers wrapped around his cock. Despite his best efforts to distract himself, he was painfully hard.

"He didn't give a shit about me when I was five. I highly doubt he would give a shit about my birthday when I'm twenty-two." Tristan smiled. It wasn't a nice smile. "He and you have something in common, you know." His fingers tightened around Zach's cock.

"What?" Zach managed, his eyes rolling to the back of his head.

"He's a high-handed prick. I later found out he's an earl." Tristan chuckled. "Anyway, he was married but couldn't keep his prick out of my mom. She was real pretty." Tristan stroked Zach's cock slowly. "I know you think I'm pretty. I look a lot like her—before she got sick." Tristan laughed. "At least you can't knock me up."

Zach stared at him.

Then he flipped them over and pressed his lips against Tristan's gently.

Tristan went still, his grip on Zach's cock loosening.

Zach kissed him softly, again and again, the kiss very innocent compared to the things they'd done in the past month.

Christ, such a sweet mouth.

Sweetest in the world.

Tristan made a small noise and broke the kiss. Squeezing Zach's cock hard, he glared. "What do you think you're doing? I'm not your bloody girlfriend. Just hurry up and fuck me."

Zach did. Of course he did.

As he buried his face in Tristan's neck and pushed inside him, he could almost relate to that asshole who had gotten Tristan's mother pregnant.

If Tristan's mother had been half as intoxicating as her son...to Zach's shame and disgust, he could understand the guy.

There was a difference, though. It was clear that at some point Tristan's father had stopped.

Zach was no longer sure he could.

Chapter 17

As far as birthdays went, this one wasn't so bad after all. Tristan's body ached pleasantly after the sex and the second training session, but a long, hot bath filled with aromatic salts refreshed him.

When he emerged from the bathroom, he was surprised to find Zach lounging on the couch in front of the TV.

"I thought you already left," he said.

Zach glanced at him. "I promised my sister I'd pick her up from work and drive her to Oxford. She works close by. It's pointless to drive home only to drive back in an hour."

Tristan padded closer and hesitated. He never knew how to act around Zach at moments like this: when they were neither training nor going to fuck. It had been so difficult to find the right balance lately, the lines getting blurred.

He could tell he wasn't the only one struggling with it.

When they weren't having sex, Zach mostly acted around him as he always did—slightly mocking, slightly cynical, and bossy—but sometimes, his behavior was...off. Tristan didn't even mean those moments when they lay next to each other after sex, sated and blissed out, and Zach would run his fingers along Tristan's spine, stroke his nape, his sweaty hair. People said and did stupid things after sex. But it wasn't just during the sex.

Zach *stared* at him. It didn't happen all that often, but when it did, it made Tristan feel funny on the inside. He didn't like the feeling—because he was absolutely addicted to it. And the worst part was, he couldn't even blame Zach for the hot and cold treatment: sometimes he felt so needy for Zach's touch that he found himself stepping closer to him when they weren't having sex. Then he realized what he was doing and lashed out at Zach with unnecessarily scathing remarks.

Fuck. This thing should have never lasted as long as it did. It had been almost a month already. He never fucked the same guy for so long. Who was he kidding? Before Zach he had never fucked the same guy *twice*.

"Are you going to stand there all evening?" Zach said, without looking at him. He had his hands propped behind his head in that universal guy gesture, looking casual, relaxed and very male.

Tristan caught his lip between his teeth, glancing at the free space next to Zach, and strode determinedly to the couch. He plopped down next to Zach. "What are you watching?"

"Back to the Future."

Tristan scrunched up his nose. "Boring."

"I didn't ask for your opinion."

Tristan lounged back, balancing his leg on his knee. His bare foot pressed against Zach's leg. "But it's boring. It's my birthday and I wanna watch something else."

Tristan hid his smile, aware he sounded like a spoiled toddler. He didn't give a shit and knew that Zach didn't, either: Zach didn't expect him to act any different. Living down to Zach's expectations was always fun. With Zach, he could be as immature and mean as he wanted. He didn't have to be nice, good-natured and laid back. He didn't have to pretend. He didn't have to be anything. It felt…different. Liberating. It felt good.

"There's another TV in the house," Zach said, his eyes still on the screen.

Tristan pursed his lips, feeling kind of annoyed that Zach wasn't paying him attention. He pressed his foot more firmly against Zach's leg.

Without sparing him a glance, Zach caught his foot.

"Stop squirming." He didn't remove his hand. Zach's thumb started stroking the bottom of his foot, absent-mindedly.

Squirming, Tristan couldn't stop a giggle from escaping his lips. He was ticklish, always had been.

Zach snatched his hand away.

Tristan stopped smiling. He shot a sideways glance at Zach and bit his lip.

"I'm bored," he said, rapping his knuckles on the wooden arm of the couch. Loudly.

He did it for a full two minutes (yep, he did count; sue him) before Zach finally let out a sigh of exasperation. Zach reached out and grabbed his hand.

"Be quiet." He put Tristan's hand on Tristan's thigh, holding it in place with his own hand.

Tristan stared at Zach's hand covering his own and then at Zach's arm around him.

Oh.

Zach's arm stiffened, as though he only now realized that he was effectively embracing Tristan.

A few tense seconds passed. Zach clearly didn't know what the hell he should do about the situation he'd gotten himself into.

His lips twitching, Tristan turned his hand so they were palm to palm. "Aww," he mock-cooed, interlacing their fingers. "Be still my heart! I think I'm going to swoon!"

"You have a heart?" Zach said, his voice laced with amusement. His arm relaxed.

"It's okay," Tristan said, squeezing Zach's fingers. "I know you can't help it."

Slowly, Zach turned his head to him. "What?"

Tristan nodded. "It's really okay. I told you I'm irresistible."

Zach shook his head. "You're—"

"Witty, brilliant, hot?"

Chuckling, Zach shot him an amused look. "Do you feel in love when you look at your reflection?"

Grinning, Tristan put his head on the back of the couch, his face only inches away from Zach's now. "You think I'm narcissistic?"

Zach gave him a strange stare.

"You tick most boxes."

Tristan gazed at him lazily. "Maybe. But aren't all people narcissistic? I think Freud said so. The difference is only one of degree."

He received another indecipherable look from Zach.

Zach lifted his hand—the one that wasn't clutched in Tristan's fingers—and brushed his knuckles against Tristan's cheek.

Tristan froze, unsure.

"You're arrogant, self-confident and haughty," Zach said. "But…" His gray eyes roamed over Tristan's face. "Sometimes I think you actually have low self-esteem and all your prickliness is just a defense mechanism."

Tristan opened his mouth but closed it without saying anything.

"Well, you're wrong," he said at last. Aware how lame his denial sounded, he scowled.

Zach looked down at his scowling mouth and kissed it lightly.

"Stop making this ridiculous face," Zach said before sucking on his lip. "Give me your tongue."

Tristan did. Somehow—he wasn't sure how—his arms ended up around Zach's neck and he was kissing back.

Somewhere in the back of his mind, an alarm bell rang. Tristan ignored it, sucking on Zach's tongue and making small noises of pleasure. God, so good. The feel, the taste, the scent…it made him giddy and warm. So warm.

The alarm went off again and Tristan dazedly realized why: they were just *kissing*, with no sex on the menu. This was getting too weird. This whole thing between them had been confusing enough already. This felt almost as weird as the feather-soft kisses Zach had given him in the afternoon after Tristan had told him about his father. Almost.

Tristan could feel the weirdness now, too, hanging in the air between them as Zach broke the kiss to nuzzle behind his ear, the tenderness of his touches contrasting with Zach's firm grip on Tristan's hips.

Burying his fingers in Zach's hair, Tristan dragged him back to his mouth, wanting more kisses. Zach obliged, kissing him thoroughly.

Zach's cell phone went off.

They ignored it.

The phone didn't stop ringing.

Sighing, Zach broke the kiss and answered the phone. "Yeah," he said before clearing his throat. "I'm on my way, Sandra."

Without looking at Tristan, he stood up. "I have to go. Don't forget you have a medical tomorrow morning. Be ready by nine." He turned away before turning back and leaning down to brush their lips together. "Happy birthday, dollface." He was gone before Tristan could say anything.

Still a little dazed, Tristan sagged back against the couch and touched his well-kissed lips.

Well, fuck.

Chapter 18

Tristan stared out of the side window, watching the landscape pass by as Zach drove them back to London. Since they had left the training center, the tension in the car hadn't faded. It was a living, breathing presence.

The medical had been uncomfortable enough. Jared had obviously noticed the love bites on various parts of his body—he would have had to be blind not to notice them— but he hadn't said anything, keeping his questions strictly professional. Yet he couldn't hide the frown on his face or the probing, hard looks he shot at Zach. Jared knew; Tristan was sure of that.

Normally, it wouldn't bother him that much. Jared was probably the only person of his acquaintance whom he completely trusted not to out him: Jared was gay himself and he was the definition of a "nice guy," if such a thing existed.

After the medical was over, Jared took Zach aside and told him something in a hushed, angry tone. Zach's jaw clenched, his eyes turning stormy as he listened to whatever Jared was saying to him.

For a long, tense moment, Zach didn't say anything. Finally, he nodded curtly and walked out of the room after telling Tristan that he would wait for him in the car. When Tristan demanded answers from Jared, the physician simply looked at him before informing him that tomorrow he would resume training with the rest of the squad.

Tomorrow.

That thought kept playing in his mind over and over. Tomorrow.

Tristan glanced at Zach, but he was looking at the road. Tristan looked back at the scenery. They were in the outskirts of London already. "Jared said I would start training with the squad tomorrow."

"Yes."

Tristan pushed his thumb against the glass. "So that means we're basically done."

He counted three seconds before Zach said, "Yes."

"Ah," Tristan said, drawing zigzag lines on the window with his finger. "About time. The season is almost over. I'll have just a month to recover my form and impress the coach."

"When you start training with the squad, don't rush to return to the pitch. Your problem is, you don't have patience." Zach let out an irritated grunt. "I got the car washed just this morning. Stop that."

Tristan didn't stop. "I have a lot of patience. I'm the paragon of patience."

"And I'm the Pope. This is your third groin injury in half a year. It's obvious you've been doing something wrong. I looked up the videos of your training sessions and noticed that you're too impatient and don't do a thorough warm-up before every training session."

Zach shook his head. "That's very important, Tristan.

A correct warm-up will help prepare your muscles for any activity."

Tristan drew a dog with his finger. Well, at least it was supposed to be a dog. He glanced out the window. "We aren't going to my house."

"No," Zach said. "I've got a DVD at my place. A guide to proper warm-up and a structured stretching routine. You will watch it carefully and follow the instructions to the letter when you start training without me." Zach went quiet for a moment. "I thought we had another week, but Jared disagreed. So you'll have to learn from the video."

Tristan started finger-painting the dog.

Zach let out an exasperated sigh. "Are you winding me up on purpose?"

"Eyes on the road, not on me," Tristan murmured. "I know it's hard, but I'm too young to die because you can't stop looking at me."

"Tristan—"

Tristan drummed his fingers on the window. "You're still looking at me." He could physically feel when Zach looked away.

They were silent for the rest of the ride.

When Zach finally parked the car in front of a big, beautiful house, Tristan laughed.

"You know, for someone who keeps bitching at me for being a spoiled, rich boy, that's pretty rich—pun intended. Your house is twice as big as mine. Who's the spoiled rich boy now?"

Zach got out of the car.

"I have a large family."

Tristan followed him into the house.

"They're here?"

"Not at the moment. My mother prefers to live with our aunt. My sister is married now and my brothers all have moved out, too, though they all still hang out here often enough. I'll get the DVD," Zach said before disappearing upstairs.

Tristan looked around the living room. It was large but looked lived-in and comfy. There were pictures on the low table by the couch. Mostly family pictures, but one of them was different. Tristan picked it up and stared at it. Zach had an arm around a gorgeous brunette.

So this was the famous Donna. Her tall, curvy figure looked perfect next to Zach's tall, masculine frame. They looked good together.

Tristan put the picture down and picked up another. Zach and his siblings: four brothers and a sister. They didn't all look like him, but the family resemblance was unmistakable. All of the brothers were tall, one of them clearly close to Zach's age.

Feeling eyes on him, Tristan looked up. Zach stood in the doorway, watching him.

"What?"

Shaking his head, Zach walked over and handed him a DVD.

Tristan made a face but took it. "Your siblings?"

Zach nodded, still watching him with the same strange expression. It was further tattering Tristan's already frayed nerves. Trying to keep his body relaxed, Tristan pointed at the black-haired guy to Zach's left on the picture. "I'd totally shag this one."

Zach's gaze followed his finger. He looked amused. "Ryan is a kid. He's just twenty-one."

"So what?" Tristan said, putting the picture on the table and smiling sweetly at Zach.

"I just turned twenty-two. Is he into guys?"

"Who?"

"Ryan."

Zach's eyes narrowed. "No, he isn't."

"Hmm. It doesn't matter."

"You don't want him," Zach said. "You're just trying to annoy me."

Inwardly bristling, Tristan struggled to keep his face neutral. "Why would that annoy you? Your brother is a big boy and can defend his virtue. And you're wrong. I've always had a thing for black hair and pale skin. He's hot—and he's my age." He smiled. "Now that I won't have you to entertain me, I'll have to find a new fucktoy. Why not him? He's exactly my type."

"Stay away from my brothers," Zach said in a low, dangerous voice. "I won't let you use them just to annoy me. None of them can handle you."

"And who can?" Tristan said, cocking his head. "You?"

Their breathing mixed, both swift and strained.

Zach's hands gripped Tristan's hips hard. "I don't give a shit what you do. Just stay away."

"Scared you wouldn't be able to keep your hands off me?"

"You little—"

"You know what?" Tristan said. "Let's skip the foreplay when we say awful things to each other and get mad." His fingers started unbuttoning Zach's shirt. He hoped Zach didn't notice how unsteady they were. He looked Zach in the eye. "I want to suck your cock. And then I want you to fuck me. Then we go on our own ways and never see each other again."

Zach was still.

His pupils were so blown that Tristan could barely even see the gray irises anymore.

He yanked Tristan to him.

They didn't make it to the bedroom. They did it right there, on the carpet in Zach's living room, surrounded by the pictures of his family and his gorgeous fiancée.

It was the worst sex in Tristan's life. He hated it and he hated Zach, hated the way the sex made him feel— frustrated, raw, and deeply unsatisfied, even after the spectacular orgasm that had him shuddering and digging his fingers into Zach's bare back.

Afterward, Zach said into his neck, "I'll have to get rid of the carpet now. And I liked this carpet. This is all your fault." His voice was still raspy and a little dazed. "Your fault." His lips were moving heatedly down the length of Tristan neck. Zach sucked hard on the skin above his pulse.

Tristan closed his eyes for a moment, fighting the lump in his throat. He opened them and let his hands fall from Zach's back to his own sides. "Get off me."

Zach didn't move, sinking his teeth into his skin. It hurt. God, did it hurt.

"Get out of me," Tristan whispered.

When Zach didn't move—was he actually trying to push himself deeper?—Tristan shoved him off and got to his feet, a little unsteadily. His body hurt. He didn't mind being fucked with little prep—he loved it rough—but, for some reason, this time he felt more bruised than he physically was.

Without looking at Zach, he put on his briefs and jeans.

He wrestled with the buttons of the shirt, his fingers clumsy.

It took several tries to get the first few pushed through their holes. "Fuck, fucking fuck —"

Zach pushed Tristan's hands away and started buttoning up the shirt. Of course *his* fingers weren't clumsy. Tristan watched those long, strong fingers make short work of it in silence. The silence was oppressive, like a living, heavy weight pressing in on his chest. Tristan hated it and hated Zach.

"Thanks," he said, very politely, stepping back.

Zach just shrugged. As if he didn't care at all. He looked like he had already lost interest in the conversation — him — and wanted to be anywhere but there.

"Bye," Tristan said, hating himself a little for being unable to come up with something witty and scathing.

Something flickered in Zach's eyes. "Goodbye," he said tersely, turning away and reaching for his clothes.

Tristan left.

Suppressing the urge to slam the door on his way out, he closed it quietly instead. He wouldn't give Zach the satisfaction of knowing that he was…angry. Was he angry? Was the tight feeling in his chest anger? He had no reason to be angry. He had known all along this would end soon. It was just…it was just too abrupt. He hadn't been ready. Just this morning, before driving him to the medical, Zach had spent fifteen minutes kissing him over and over, as though he couldn't get enough. And now — now, nothing. It was just too sudden. That was why he felt so off-balance; that was all.

"Hey, are you going inside or leaving?"

Tristan lifted his head.

A tall guy was smiling at him.

After a moment, Tristan recognized him from the photo.

This was the brother who looked a lot like Zach, except his hair was black. Just like Zach's, his facial features were striking rather than classically handsome. He had a different build, though: his body was lean rather than muscular. He must be in his early twenties.

The guy held his hand out. "Nick Hardaway."

Tristan clasped it briefly and put on a smile. "I'm—"

"Tristan DuVal," Nick said, flashing him an attractive grin. "A Chelsea player and Zach's current victim."

"Not anymore."

Nick's gray eyes swept over him, excitement flashing through his face. "You mean you recovered? About time!" At Tristan's startled look, Nick gave him a smile and winked. "A Chelsea fan since I was a kid. How am I doing so far? I'm trying so hard not to make a fool of myself."

Right. Zach had mentioned that one of his brothers was his fan.

Tristan smiled, letting his public mask slip into place. After five years in the spotlight, it was like a second skin to him now. It wasn't even a lie most of the time. He liked being the center of attention. He liked being liked. He liked being admired and adored by fans. It was truly easy.

"Chelsea fan?" Tristan said with a smile. "Your brother must hate you."

Grinning, Nick waggled his eyebrows. "Which one?"

Tristan chuckled. "That bad, huh?"

"Yup. I'm the black sheep of the family." He shuddered dramatically and, leaning to Tristan's ear, said in a conspiratorial, horrified voice, "They're all Gunners."

Tristan's laugh was cut short when the door opened behind him.

"What are you doing here?" Zach's voice was very cold.

Tristan tensed. Nick turned his head, his easy smile transforming into a puzzled frown. "Nice to see you, too, big bro. Who took the jam out of your doughnut? This is still my home, as you keep telling me."

"Right," Tristan said, stepping away. "I've got to go."

Nick grabbed his arm. "Hey, not so fast! I can't let you go just like that."

"Nick, we've talked about it," Zach said sharply. "You can't bother my patients."

"No problem." Nick smirked at his brother, clearly enjoying riling him up. "He's not your patient anymore."

"Nick." The warning in Zach's voice was unmistakable, and Nick's smirk faded, a look of genuine confusion appearing on his face.

Ignoring Zach, whose eyes were boring holes in the back of his head, Tristan smiled at Nick. He liked his fans. And he liked this one. And he liked pissing Zach off most of all. "I have to go now, but you can get my number from Zach. Call me."

Surprise and pleasure flashed across Nick's face. "Great, I will. See you."

Tristan nodded and walked away, refusing to look back at Zach. He knew if he did, he wouldn't be able to hold himself together. God, he was so done with it—with this weird, pathetic thing, whatever it was. Screw Zach. He was done. So done. He couldn't wait for his life to get back to normal. Zach was welcome to marry his gorgeous fiancée and live his happily ever after. Tristan didn't give a shit.

And if his throat was a little tight and painful, no one was any the wiser.

Chapter 19

"All right, lads, a break for half an hour!" the coach announced, much to the players' relief.

Kicking the ball away, Gabriel DuVal wiped the sweat off his forehead and looked around. A smile tugged at his lips when he noticed the familiar tall figure on the other end of the training pitch. Ignoring his teammates, he headed toward his…boyfriend. Boyfriend. The word still felt strange. It didn't quite fit.

"My Jared," he mouthed tentatively and smiled to himself. Much better.

He sneaked up on Jared and looped his arm around his neck.

"Hey, what are you doing?"

"Observing," Jared said, his gaze trained on the reserve players.

Gabriel paid them little mind.

He bit the inside of his cheek, trying to suppress the totally inappropriate urge to press his lips against Jared's strong jawline and suck. In a way, it was weird.

He'd always known Jared was handsome, but just a few months ago, it had been something abstract: he was straight and his love for Jared had been strictly platonic. While he was relieved that this new physical aspect of their relationship didn't feel forced, Gabriel was a little unsettled by how much he'd grown to need it. Now he couldn't get enough of Jared's body as much as he couldn't get enough of his affection and love. He wanted to kiss him.

But of course he couldn't. Most people might be used to their unusual closeness and didn't bat an eye at their displays of affections, but even they couldn't get away with a public kiss. Sometimes being a football player sucked.

"Observing what?" Gabriel said, trying to distract himself.

"Tristan," Jared replied.

Frowning, Gabriel followed Jared's gaze. His prick of a brother was a little apart from the main group, kicking the ball at his feet. "Why? I thought he was fit enough to train without medical supervision. He's playing in the next game."

"Didn't you notice anything off about him?" Jared said, stroking Gabriel's shoulder. He dropped his hand after a moment, probably remembering they had an audience.

"Nope," Gabriel said, already missing the touch.

"Look at him," Jared said.

"I'm already looking at him."

"No, look at him. Don't you see anything strange?"

His curiosity piqued, Gabriel studied his brother more carefully. Tristan was silent, his eyes downcast and jaw clenched tightly. He was giving off a distinct leave-me-alone vibe.

"He looks moody," Gabriel said before frowning. "He looks moody," he repeated slower, as the words sank in.

"Yes," Jared said. "And he's been that way the entire week—ever since he resumed training here."

Huh. Tristan never showed his temper in public. Never. He was the "nice brother." He was the one who was always in good humor, who always had a joke to say and a smile to give. Gabriel knew better than anyone that it was just a facade, but other people didn't.

As far as the public was concerned, Tristan was the ultimate good guy, a poor orphan who achieved his dreams through hard work and dedication, against all odds. It made a good story (and never mind that Gabe's story was basically the same; he wasn't the media darling). Tristan carefully guarded his reputation and was rarely seen frowning or being mean in public.

"There's something wrong with him," Jared said.

"Why should we care?" Gabriel murmured, leaning into Jared.

"Gabe," Jared said in a warning tone.

Grinning at him, Gabriel made an innocent face. "What?"

Jared didn't look amused. "We're in public."

"So what? I wanna touch you."

Jared's expression softened. "I want to touch you, too." The look in his dark blue eyes was so tender and intense at the same time, it warmed Gabe to his toes. "But it's dangerous," Jared said, turning back to Tristan.

Sighing, Gabriel straightened up. "Fine. So why should we care about Tristan's moodiness? Why should we care if he's sulking for some reason?"

Jared didn't answer immediately. "I'm worried it has something to do with Zach."

"Zach?"

Jared seemed…uncomfortable. A few seconds passed before he replied, "About a month ago, Zach came to me for advice. Well, he didn't come for that, but I gave him some advice."

Gabriel's confusion was only growing. "What sort of advice?"

"He told me he was attracted to Tristan."

"Attracted to Tristan?!"

"Hush," Jared said, a faint smile playing on his lips. "Why are you so surprised?"

"Why?" Gabriel looked at him in disbelief. "Zach's straight! He's marrying Donna in a month!"

"They're still in an open relationship," Jared reminded him. "And well, if anyone could tempt a straight man, it would be Tristan."

Gabriel's eyes narrowed, an ugly, vicious feeling twisting his insides. "Oh yeah?"

Jared laughed, shaking his head. "Silly," he said, his thumb brushing Gabriel's wrist. "You're so silly."

Gabriel blushed, embarrassed by his outburst of jealousy but unable to do anything about it.

Of course he was being silly; he knew that. He knew Jared loved him. He knew he was Jared's world as much as Jared was his. But the fear of losing Jared wasn't something he could rationalize away.

"What advice did you give him?" he asked, curling his fingers around Jared's biceps. Screw it; he didn't care if anyone decided it was too gay.

"I told him Donna deserved his full attention and he should get Tristan out of his system before the wedding. In other words, I told him to fuck Tristan and get over it."

"Ew," Gabriel said. "I really, really didn't need that mental image. But anyway, what's the problem?"

Jared's expression was grim. "They're both adults, but Tristan is my patient—well, not now, but he is. I feel a bit guilty that I didn't think about Tristan's feelings when I gave Zach that advice."

Gabriel laughed. "Feelings? He doesn't have feelings. Come on, do you think Tristan got emotionally attached after a fuck?"

"That's the thing," Jared said, not sharing his amusement. "It wasn't just a fuck. When Tristan came for his medical, he was covered in hickeys."

Okay, now that was something he really didn't need to know.

"Gross," he said. "So why is that a problem, exactly?"

Jared had a pinched look on his face. "I gave Zach that advice a month ago, Gabe. I thought it would be just a fuck, to scratch the itch. I didn't think it would last so long. When people fuck for weeks, it's hard to keep things no strings attached." Guilt flashed through his blue eyes. "Like Oscar did and then he got hurt when he realized it would always be you for me." Jared pressed his lips together. "That wasn't what I had in mind when I gave Zach that advice."

"How do you know it was Zach who gave him the hickeys? Maybe Tristan slept around later."

"I know it was Zach. I observed them together. Their body language said it all. I don't think they looked away from each other for more than a few seconds." Jared smiled crookedly. "It was a little awkward to be in the room with them."

Gabriel returned his gaze to his brother. "You really think Tristan got attached?" The mere idea of it seemed ridiculous. Tristan didn't get attached to people.

"I hope not," Jared said. "But—well, look at him."

"Maybe it's totally unrelated to Zach." Gabriel scoffed. "Tristan has an icicle instead of a heart. Last year, when you were—when you were *gone*, he made fun of me, told me my moping was pathetic. He wouldn't recognize an emotion if it hit him in the face."

"Maybe that's the problem," Jared said thoughtfully.

Gabe sighed. He could see how much it was bothering Jared that he might have inadvertently hurt one of his patients. Jared was too damn nice to people who didn't deserve it and paid them too much attention (In Gabe's opinion, he was the only person who should have Jared's attention, but it was neither here nor there).

"All right," he said, touching Jared's shoulder. "If you really feel guilty about it, I'll go talk to him and find out what's bothering him, mhm?"

Jared's proud look made him feel about ten feet tall.

Turning away to hide his blush of embarrassment, Gabe strode toward his brother.

"Hey."

Tristan completely ignored him, his gaze on the ball at his feet.

Gabriel studied him in silence.

When they were teenagers, he used to envy Tristan's flawless skin and grace. Even now, with the dark scowl marring his features, Tristan looked pretty much flawless. Still, he had trouble imagining Tristan and Zach together. Zach was the last person he had expected to be fooled by Tristan's exterior.

At last, Tristan shot him a look. "What do you want?"

Gabriel decided to cut to the chase. He didn't want to be talking to Tristan longer than necessary. "I want you to tell me you don't have a thing for Zach."

If he hadn't been watching so carefully, he would have missed the barely noticeable stiffening in Tristan's posture.

Tristan chuckled, a bright, amused smile appearing on his lips. "Don't be an idiot. Me? I fucked him a few times. It's over now. Good riddance. It was getting boring."

If he hadn't grown up watching Tristan tell a lie with a straight face, he would have bought it. But he had. And this bright smile was the one Tristan reserved for hopeless situations, when he needed to bullshit his way out of them.

But…did it matter? Tristan's answer was the one he had wanted to hear. He could leave now. It wasn't like he really cared whether Tristan was upset or not. There were a few people Gabe cared for and Tristan wasn't one of them.

He could leave. He could pretend he'd believed Tristan. He could. He probably should.

Except…except he couldn't.

The problem was, since early childhood, Tristan had been the only constant in his life. They didn't like each other, but he could always count on Tristan to remain the same self-centered, unfeeling dick. And seeing Tristan actually upset made him…uneasy, like the sky suddenly turned green.

"You're lying," he said.

A startled look crossed Tristan's face, as if he didn't expect Gabe to call him out on his bullshit, but the next moment, it was gone. "Don't confuse me with you," Tristan said. "I'm not you. I'm not stupid like you."

Gabriel lowered his voice. "If you mean Jared—"

"Of course I mean Jared. Look at you." A sneer curled Tristan's lips. "All wrapped up in a man who will throw you away when he finds something better."

Gabriel let out a laugh. "Yeah, right. Jared loves me."

Tristan cocked his head, his expression almost pitying. "Now? Maybe yes. But you're stupid if you think it will last forever. In a year or two, Jared will wake up and realize you're not good enough. Because you aren't and you never will be. And it will wreck you when he leaves you." Tristan's eyes held his. "Admit it: deep down, you know he will leave. That's why you're scared of losing him. You know people like us don't get a happily ever after. I'm fine with it, because I don't need it. I don't need anyone. You used to be the same way, but now you..." Tristan gave him a look of disdain. "You were a pathetic, hollow shell while he was out of your life for a few months. What are you going to do when he leaves you for good? You're such an idiot, Gabe."

Gabriel bit out, "At least I'm not a pathetic, hollow shell all the time. At least I'm not a fucking coward."

Tristan's face went completely blank.

Gabriel stalked away, balling his hands into fists.

He told himself to ignore Tristan's words. They had been aimed to hurt, to plant a seed of doubt; he knew that. Tristan was excellent at finding a weakness and hitting where it hurt the most.

But his words kept ringing in his ears, over and over and over.

In a year or two, Jared will wake up and realize you're not good enough. Deep down, you know he will leave. You know people like us don't get a happily ever after.

His jaw clenched, he made his way into the training facility.

"Gabe!" Jared's voice startled him.

Gabriel blinked owlishly when he was pushed into the nearest room and Jared's concerned eyes peered at him.

"What's wrong, Gab—"

Gabe kissed him desperately, looping his arms around him and holding on as tightly as he could. "I love you, I love you, I love you," he whispered between frantic kisses before burying his face in the hollow of Jared's neck.

Jared's arms tightened around him, and God, it felt so perfect and right, but it hurt. It hurt.

For a long time, Jared didn't say anything, simply stroking his hair.

"What is this about?" he said after a while. "Is it Tristan?"

Gabriel laughed roughly. "I know I should never listen to him, but—but I'm scared that—I *know* he's right."

"About what?"

"That one day you'll realize I'm not good enough for you," he muttered, barely audibly. "No one loves me. I don't get why you still do."

Jared sighed and, taking his chin in his hand, forced Gabriel to meet his eyes. His blue eyes were amused and tender at the time. "I'm well aware of all the…less than charming aspects of your personality. I've seen you at your worst. I've seen you be selfish, mean, vindictive and overly possessive. And it doesn't make me love you less."

"Why?" he whispered.

"Because when you love someone, you don't love them for their good personality traits and actions. You love them because you love them, with all their flaws and ridiculous insecurities." Jared smiled, touching Gabriel's lip. "I love you, baby. Probably more than I should."

Gabriel smiled back and hid his smile in Jared's neck, hugging him tightly. He closed his eyes, feeling the ever-present fear finally dissipate, washed away by a surge of emotion.

Tristan was wrong. Maybe he wasn't good, but he

was good enough for the person who mattered the most. The key was finding that person.

And suddenly, he felt incredibly sorry for his brother. Tristan would never have this, because he wasn't brave enough to want it. Wasn't brave enough to ask.

"So what about Tristan?" Jared said, as if reading his thoughts. "Is he upset about Zach?"

Making a face, Gabriel pulled back a little to look at Jared. "Jay, when I asked him if he had a thing for Zach, Tristan hit me in my weakest spot and almost reduced me to tears. For Tristan, that's practically a declaration of love."

A crease appeared between Jared's brows. "And now what?"

"Nothing," Gabriel said, hating a little how well he understood Tristan. "Whatever he feels, it doesn't matter, because he hates it." Maybe Tristan didn't have an icicle instead of a heart, but for him emotions were a weakness, and Tristan's sense of self-preservation was unrivaled. Gabriel met Jared's concerned eyes.

"Don't worry," he said, straightening Jared's collar. "Nothing will happen. He'll stay away from Zach and eventually his heart will freeze again, like in that fairy tale." He smiled at his own bad joke because Jared didn't. Sighing, Gabriel carded his fingers through Jared's hair. "Don't worry, really. Zach will marry Donna, and Tristan will be back to being an insufferable prick—not that he still isn't an insufferable prick."

Jared didn't look particularly reassured. "And if he doesn't stay away?"

"He will," Gabe said. "Tristan once told me he would walk over anyone to get what he wanted, but the thing is, if he wants something too much, it scares him shitless and he runs in the opposite direction."

Gabriel smiled crookedly. "Yep, that's how fucked up he is. Do you think he's more fucked up than me?"

Smiling, Jared kissed him on the nose. "Unlikely."

Gabe just laughed and didn't deny it. He might be a fucked up person, but at least he was a very happy one.

Chapter 20

As Tristan sat on the couch next to Zach's brother, in Zach's living room, watching Zach's TV and drinking Zach's beer, he wondered what the fuck he was doing.

He wanted to kick himself, but mostly he blamed Gabriel. It was Gabe's fault for getting him so riled up yesterday that when Nick Hardaway called and asked if they could hang out, Tristan agreed without thinking. When Nick had said he was at Zach's place, Tristan should have definitely told him that they couldn't hang out there. But he didn't, and now here he was. Idiot.

To make things more complicated, Nick's arm was draped over the back of the couch, his fingers not quite touching Tristan's shoulder.

Tristan wasn't naive. He could see that Nick was half-besotted with him already. The only thing preventing Nick from making a move on him was probably his celebrity status. Nick was cautious—as he should be, since Tristan was supposedly straight, as all footballers supposedly were—but Tristan knew it wouldn't last.

He hadn't known the guy long, but he could see it wasn't in Nick's nature to be cautious.

The guy was the definition of reckless; he didn't seem to take anything seriously. He was also an unashamed flirt.

Tristan was still undecided what to do about it. He should probably pretend to be straight and gently turn him down—it was safer that way. But a part of him—the part that was responsible for encouraging their acquaintance—wanted to see Zach's face when he realized Tristan was fucking his brother. And it pissed Tristan off. He wasn't supposed to care about Zach's reaction. Zach was his ex-physiotherapist. He was just a guy he'd had a fling with. The guy who was getting married in a month. Zach didn't like him, and the sentiment was entirely mutual. He didn't give a shit about Zach.

He hadn't seen Zach in eight days.

Disgusted with the direction his thoughts had taken (again), Tristan tried to focus on the movie they were watching, but those idiotic thoughts refused to go away completely, buzzing at the back of his mind.

Jesus Christ on a stick.

These days, it felt like he had a split personality. His stupid self had a one-track mind. His normal self cringed every time he caught himself thinking about Zach's hands, his mouth, his warmth, his arms around him, his scent. The scent thing was the most ridiculous part. For heaven's sake, he never noticed how people smelled—unless they smelled badly.

He was going mad. Just yesterday, he snapped at one of the team therapists for massaging him wrongly only because he wanted Zach's hands on him. God, he felt like bitch-slapping himself. He was turning into Gabe—*worse*, actually, since Gabe was at least all pathetic over a man who gave a shit about him; Tristan couldn't say the same about Zach.

Nick's thumb brushed his neck, getting him back to the present.

Tristan chewed on his lip. Maybe he should encourage Nick. Why not? The guy was handsome and eager to get into his pants, and it was unlikely he would spread any rumors: he didn't seem the type. And it would be good for him to fuck someone other than Zach. Jesus, he couldn't even *remember* what it felt like to have sex with someone else. A month of non-stop sex with one man had clearly messed with his head.

"I'm curious about something," Nick said suddenly.

Tristan turned his head to him. "Yeah?"

Nick's eyes swept over his face, searching for something. "Why is Zach angry at you?"

Tristan didn't have to feign his surprise. "He is?"

Nick laughed a little. "He bit my head off when I asked for your number. I felt about two inches tall." He winced, although his eyes were still full of amusement. "I'm not ashamed to admit Zach scares me when he's angry. It's a Pavlovian response. I can't help it." He grinned. "I actually had to sneak into his room to get your number while he was in the shower." He looked at Tristan through heavy-lidded eyes. "But it was totally worth it."

Tristan smiled back, unsure what to say. The guy really was very attractive. In the dim light, he looked even more like—

No, he *wasn't* going there.

The silence stretched. Nick's hand dropped on Tristan's neck and his lips were suddenly much closer.

Tristan tensed, but before he could decide what to do, the front door opened.

"Are we interrupting something?"

Tristan's stomach plummeted to his feet.

Zach stood by the door with his arm around a gorgeous woman.

Refusing to meet Zach's eyes, Tristan focused his gaze on the woman. Donna.

"Hey, Donna," Nick said lazily, waving at the couple with the hand that wasn't around Tristan's neck. "You're back?"

The woman—Donna—smiled. Even her smile was gorgeous. She and Zach really made a beautiful couple: both of them tall, confident, and striking.

"Hi, Nick," she said before looking at Tristan. Her sharp, dark eyes definitely didn't miss Nick's hand on Tristan's neck. She smiled wider. "I see you're being rude, as always. Are you going to introduce me to your…friend?"

"This is Tristan," Nick said with a grin and a bit of an eye-roll. "Tris, this is the poor woman who agreed to marry my bore of a brother."

"Nice to meet you," Donna said with genuine pleasure in her voice.

Tristan nodded with a bright smile. "Likewise."

"What are you doing here?" Zach said. His voice sounded a little strange.

Tristan didn't look his way.

"Your eyes are failing you at your advanced age," Nick told his brother. "We're watching a movie."

"I wasn't talking to you," Zach said. "Tristan."

Reluctantly, he dragged his gaze to Zach.

He wasn't prepared for the greedy way Zach's eyes took him in, or the way he was immediately assaulted by a disgusting wave of emotions and needs.

God, it wasn't fair.

How could a man look so good? Zach's lean cheeks were clean-shaven, drawing attention to his strong jawline and firm, sensual lips. Lips he'd tasted. Lips that had tasted him everywhere.

Zach's eyes shifted to his brother's hand on Tristan's neck, his body giving off anger like rolling waves battering an unprotected shore. Tristan could almost smell the testosterone coming off him. He had to shake the totally ridiculous urge to push Nick away.

Their gazes clashed and locked. Zach's eyes were *blazing*.

"What?" Tristan managed.

"You forgot the DVD I wanted you to watch," Zach said tersely. "Come with me." And he headed upstairs, confident that Tristan would follow him. Ugh. Tristan had almost forgotten about his high-handed ways.

He wasn't going. He wasn't. Zach wasn't even his personal trainer anymore.

Zach stopped at the top of the stairs and pinned him with a look. "Come with me. Now."

Nick said something, but Tristan could barely hear him. He stood and followed Zach upstairs, angry with himself. He couldn't believe he was doing what Zach wanted, like a—like a dog wagging its tail for a bone. Unbelievable.

Zach was waiting for him on the second floor. He had his arms crossed over his chest, the look on his face positively murderous.

"I told you to stay away from my brothers." His voice was deceptively low and calm.

Tristan crossed his arms, subconsciously mirroring Zach's posture.

"So what? You have no right to tell me what to do. You're nothing to me and I'm nothing to you."

"Nick isn't nothing to me."

Tristan chuckled. "So you're worried about your brother? What a wonderful brother you are, saving him from my evil clutches. Don't worry, sex didn't kill anyone yet."

"Sex?"

Tristan cocked his head, holding his gaze. "He's better than you, you know. Unlike you, he can go at it for hours."

Zach stared at him for a moment before his lips curled up. "You really think I'm going to buy it?"

"I don't care if you buy it or not." Tristan shrugged. "Couldn't care less what you think. Now, if you excuse me, Nick is waiting for me—"

"You will not sleep with him."

Tristan blinked slowly. Then he narrowed his eyes. "Excuse me?"

Zach looked irritated, as though he already regretted saying it. Nevertheless, he repeated, "You will not sleep with him."

If Tristan were a cartoon character, there would have been steam coming out of his ears. "I will not?" he said, very softly.

"You will not," Zach said.

Tristan opened his mouth and closed it soundlessly.

Then, he stepped closer and cupped Zach's cheek with his hand.

Zach stiffened.

It was so quiet here. Or was their breathing just that loud?

Leaning in, Tristan brushed his lips against Zach's clean-shaven jaw. Zach's body went rigid with tension. Inhaling shallowly, Tristan dragged his quivering lips across Zach's chin, feeling Zach's ragged, hot breath on his skin. He stopped when their lips were an inch apart.

A beat passed.

Tristan smiled and whispered,

"Fuck you, Zach."

When he pulled away, the withering look Zach shot him was almost worth his weak knees and raging hard-on. Almost.

"Your touching concern for your brother is duly noted," he grated out before stalking off.

Chapter 21

As Tristan disappeared out of sight, Zach closed his eyes, trying to pull himself together.

He had managed to stay away for the past eight days and now the brat had undone all the hard work with one not-quite-touch. Zach grimaced. The fact that he knew exactly how many days it had been was bloody ridiculous. He was thirty years old. A grown man, not a schoolboy. It shouldn't have been such a struggle to keep away.

But it was.

He used to consider himself a rational, cool-headed man. Used to. He had thought it would be easier when Tristan was no longer around to drive him crazy, but it was actually worse. Because when Tristan had been around, he could at least blame his weakness on Tristan's pretty eyes, and lips, and that maddening smirk.

With the boy out of sight, Zach had no excuse for thinking about him non-stop, wanting to see him, and just *wanting*. He had found himself thinking of Tristan's scowling lips whenever he jerked off, and remembering the way those aquamarine eyes got glazed with need when Zach moved inside of him.

For fuck's sake.

It had been eight days.

He hadn't seen Donna in over a month while she was in China and he'd barely thought of her.

Donna.

Zach sighed. He wasn't looking forward to their conversation.

Of course he wasn't going to lie to her, but even thinking about explaining this thing to Donna made him wish she hadn't returned from China yet. He knew she had noticed straight away back at the airport that his mood was off. She hadn't called him out on it, but she had been observing him thoughtfully. She knew him; of course she hadn't missed how agitated he was.

Taking a deep breath and glancing down to make sure his arousal wasn't noticeable, Zach followed Tristan downstairs.

"Something wrong?" Donna murmured, touching his arm. She pulled him toward the kitchen, clearly wishing to talk. She stopped when he didn't budge. "Zach?"

"Let's watch the movie," he said, pulling her toward the unoccupied couch.

"Oh, come on!" Nick said with an eye-roll. "We don't need babysitters. We promise not to spill things on your couch if you leave us alone." He wiggled his eyebrows with a grin.

Zach clenched his fingers into a fist.

Donna chuckled. "Don't look at me. Blame your brother."

"You heard that, right?" Nick said, giving Zach the get-the-hell-out-of-here-and-stop-cockblocking-me look.

Zach chose to pretend he didn't understand it. "This is my house," he said, making his way to the mini-bar to pull out two beer bottles. He opened them and returned to the couch. "If you don't like my rules, go somewhere else."

"Okay," Nick said slowly.

Nick and Donna shared a look.

Zach pretended not to notice and handed Donna one of the bottles.

"So what are we watching?" Donna asked, trying to break the sudden tension in the room.

Nick said something and Donna laughed and said something back.

Tristan didn't make a sound.

Zach took a seat beside Donna, focused his eyes on the screen, and tried to relax.

"Are you going to tell me what's wrong with you?" Donna murmured, keeping her voice low, though he didn't know why she bothered: their voices were masked by the sound of explosions.

"What are you talking about?"

"I'm talking about the fact that we're watching an action flick—and you hate action flicks—with your little brother and his boyfriend, and we could have been doing something far more interesting." Her fingers ran down his chest lightly. "You're so tense. Did you get laid at all while I was away?"

"He's not Nick's boyfriend. He's my former patient."

Donna blinked and looked at him oddly.

"I know who he is," she said after a moment. "Of course I know. What self-respecting sports journalist wouldn't recognize Tristan DuVal? But they look pretty chummy to me. Look at them."

Zach didn't want to. But he had little choice now.

Nick had his arm draped over the back of the couch behind Tristan's head, the tips of his fingers touching Tristan's shoulder.

Zach's grip on the bottle tightened.

"Zach?" she said.

Nick's thumb was inches away from the spot below Tristan's ear—the spot that made Tristan shiver and moan whenever Zach brushed his lips against it.

"Zach?"

Had Nick touched him there?

"Zach!" She pinched him.

He snapped his gaze back to Donna. "What?"

She frowned before glancing at Tristan. "I feel like I'm missing something. What's going on?"

Zach took a big gulp from his beer, wishing it was something stronger. "Nothing."

"Then why do you look like you want to hit someone?" Donna touched his stiff arm. "What's wrong with you?"

He couldn't lie to her.

"I slept with him."

In his peripheral vision, he could see Donna's mouth falling open.

"Ah," she said at last.

He looked at her, surprised by the discomfort in her voice. She had never reacted this way when they talked about their flings.

She smiled a little, but he knew her. His confession made her uneasy.

Zach frowned. Donna wasn't homophobic. She had known for ages that Nick was gay, and she had been always supportive of him.

"You're uncomfortable," he said.

She didn't bother denying it.

She winced, looking embarrassed. "Sorry. You know I'm not like that, but…"

She chuckled, shaking her head.

"Dammit. I'm a modern, open-minded woman. I don't know why this...God, this is silly. I'm not bigoted. I'm not. It shouldn't matter—"

"But it does," Zach said quietly. In a way, he understood. He didn't hold it against her. It was one thing to be open-minded when it concerned someone else, but when it concerned the man she was going to marry...There were certain unflattering stereotypes about gay men. All of them were bullshit, as far as Zach was concerned. However, not everyone shared that view.

"I don't think less of you," she said quickly. "There's nothing wrong with it. I don't mind you sleeping with other *people*—it doesn't matter if it's a man or a woman. No difference to me."

She wasn't being entirely truthful, but Zach chose not to say anything.

She was clearly uncomfortable by the fact that she was uncomfortable. Donna had always prided herself on being open-minded, practical and unprejudiced. And if she wanted to pretend that thinking about Zach in bed with another man wasn't distasteful to her, he wasn't going to argue.

"You just surprised me, I guess," she said. "You never told me you were attracted to men, too."

"Because I'm not usually attracted to men," Zach said, rubbing his brow. "I experimented a bit in college before we got together, but it wasn't really my thing. He's—he was the exception."

"Why?"

Leaning back against the couch, Zach sipped his beer and smiled. "You have eyes. Can't you guess?"

"Bollocks," she said. "You've worked with hundreds of handsome men before."

Zach shrugged. "He just gets under my skin." This was the understatement of the century. He took a swig from the bottle. "It doesn't matter now. I slept with him. Past tense."

"Past tense? Then why are you bothered that your brother is all over him?"

"I'm not bothered."

"Right," she said flatly. "If I didn't know better, I'd think you were jealous."

The muscles in Zach's jaw worked, heat rushing to his face. "Nick doesn't know who he's dealing with. Tristan will walk all over him."

"Nick is twenty-three and can take care of himself. You've never cared who he has sex with."

"There's no sex," he bit off.

He could feel her eyes on him, probing and assessing.

"You still want him," she said at last. She didn't sound angry—just surprised and more than a little disconcerted. Of course she was disconcerted: this wasn't something that ever happened before. They were in a long-term relationship, sometimes they got laid while they were apart, and then they got back and joked about it together: that was how it was supposed to work. That was how their relationship *had* worked for ten years. Most people didn't understand how they could be okay with a non-exclusive relationship, but it worked for them. It worked for them because they knew there were no feelings involved when they slept with other people. They knew they were the endgame for each other.

Neither of them was supposed to get hung up on somebody else. Especially not when their wedding was a month away.

"You still want him," she repeated quieter. "Zach—"

Zach put the bottle on the floor. "It doesn't matter. It's just lust. I can control it."

Liar, a voice whispered in the back of his mind. *Liar, liar, liar.*

Chapter 22

At this rate, Tristan was going to have a multiple personality disorder.

He tried very hard to ignore the couple on the other couch. He tried hard to focus on the movie and the hot guy seated next to him. It didn't work. Instead, he couldn't help thinking of the quiet evening just a week ago when he'd been the one curled up against Zach as they watched the movie together. There was a horrible feeling in the pit of his stomach that just wouldn't go away. He wanted to punch something. He wanted to be anywhere but here. He wanted to shove Donna off the couch, snuggle up to Zach, and press his bare foot against Zach's thigh. He wanted to hear Zach say something sardonic while Zach's hand stroked his foot. He wanted Zach to—

Tristan cut the train of thought, furious with himself.

His gaze strayed to the other couch again. Zach and his girlfriend were no longer talking. They both seemed deep in thought.

His eyes lingered on Zach. He licked his lips. They missed Zach's.

The craving was so intense, his mouth almost ached with it. Jesus, what was *wrong* with him? It was bad enough that he missed the sex; craving Zach's kisses just made him an idiot. He was done with Zach. He should have never fucked him in the first place. Taken, straight guys had "bad idea" written all over them. It didn't matter that Zach was still technically in an open relationship; soon he would be just hers.

The diamond on Donna's finger caught the light. Tristan looked away, curling his own fingers.

"Do you want to leave?" Nick said suddenly. His hand dropped onto Tristan's shoulder again. "We can do something more interesting."

Before he could decide what to say, the front door opened again.

"Hey, look at this! Why weren't we invited to Family Night?"

The newcomers were two guys about Tristan's age. Tristan recognized the guy who had spoken. It was Zach's brother, Ryan— the very handsome one, with dark hair and green eyes.

"You mean you?" the other guy said, elbowing him with a grin. "Last time I checked my surname wasn't Hardaway."

Grinning back, Ryan pulled him into a headlock. "Aw, come on, Grayson! You know you love being an honorary member of our family."

Tristan went still. He could barely hear their banter with Nick. He stared at the guy Ryan had called Grayson.

Grayson was a common surname.

It was a very common surname. London was huge.

The odds were ridiculous.

But it was possible.

The guy was the right age—and blond.

When the guy sauntered closer, grinning and trading jokes with the Hardaway brothers, Tristan inhaled shakily. The guy's eyes were just like his.

"This clumsy git spilled coffee on my laptop, so we wanted to grab my old one until I fix it," Ryan said.

Nick chuckled. "You two are gayer than me. 'We,' huh?"

"What can I say?" Smiling, Ryan slung an arm around Grayson's shoulders. "He's mad about me. I feel sorry for him, so I let him tag along." He grinned at Grayson and gave him a loud, sloppy kiss on the cheek. "Right, Jamie?"

Tristan swallowed, any remaining doubts he'd had now gone. Jamie. James. James Grayson.

His brother.

"Don't call me that," James said with a wince before laughing. "If Dad hears you calling me Jamie, he'll—"

"Give me the glare of doom, I know." Ryan grinned. "I'm not exactly his Lordship's favorite person in the world."

Tristan's stomach clenched.

He stared at them, trying to reconcile this attractive smiling guy with the ugly, whiny boy he remembered him as.

He nearly laughed when he realized why he couldn't. All those years ago, his childish mind had built up his brother into a little monster James wasn't. Because it was easier to hate something bad and repulsive. That way, it was easier to pretend Tristan was better.

Well, it was obvious he wasn't.

As he watched James laugh and joke with the Hardaway brothers, looking so *at home*, Tristan felt nausea rise up his throat.

He could never be so effortlessly friendly. He could never be so easy-going and good-natured. Ultimately, James seemed to be the guy Tristan pretended to be. There was probably some irony there. Somewhere.

When James said something that made even Zach grin—Zach had never smiled at *him* like that—Tristan's stomach twisted into hard, painful knots. A wave of deja vu hit him hard and he was a five-year-old boy again, staring at the closed door that separated him from being the boy he could never be.

Feeling sick, Tristan stood up and muttered, "I have to go." He didn't care if the others had heard him—or noticed.

* * *

Zach snapped his eyes to Tristan when he suddenly strode toward the door.

"Hey, where are you going?" Nick said, jumping to his feet and following him. He grabbed Tristan's shoulder.

Flinching, Tristan glowered at him. "Leave me alone!"

Nick staggered back, shock plain on his face. Of course he was shocked. Nick didn't know Tristan as Zach knew him. Nick had never seen Tristan throw a temper tantrum.

Except this wasn't a mere temper tantrum. Tristan's eyes looked haunted, and for a moment he seemed incredibly fragile before he turned away and stalked out of the house.

A stunned silence descended on the room.

Nick moved to follow Tristan.

"No," Zach said sharply. "I'll talk to him."

Nick glanced at the front door. "But—"

Zach was already moving, ignoring the looks his brothers and Donna were giving him.

Once outside, he strode toward Tristan, who was walking to his car slowly, like an old man. A flash of concern washed over Zach. Had Tristan hurt his groin again?

"Tristan!"

Tristan gave no outward sign that he had heard him.

Frowning, Zach caught up to him and turned him around. He half-expected that Tristan would lash out as he did at Nick, but instead he stared at Zach with the same haunted look in his eyes before saying in a hostile tone, "Why are you here? Did Nick send you to deal with the crazy guy?"

"No one sent me," Zach said, searching Tristan's face for a clue. His voice softened. "What is it, brat?"

Something in Tristan's expression shattered. The next thing he knew, he had Tristan's face in the crook of his neck and Tristan's arms around him, hugging him like a lifeline. Zach would have been less startled if he had seen an elephant in his backyard. He stood still, all his senses assaulted by Tristan's proximity. "Tristan—"

"Shut up," Tristan whispered. "Shut up, shut up, shut up."

"Okay," Zach said, his hands twitching by his sides. Finally, he gave in to his desire and wrapped his arms around Tristan, pulling him closer.

A peculiar small noise tore out of Tristan's throat. "I hate you," he said into his neck. "Tighter."

Christ.

What was wrong with him?

Zach tightened his embrace, closing his eyes. How could someone so prickly feel so good in his arms? Gritting his teeth in annoyance—with himself more than with Tristan—he buried his face in Tristan's hair. He inhaled greedily, trying to make sense of his conflicting emotions. Protectiveness. Disgust with how easily Tristan got under his skin and made him want to do whatever Tristan wanted. Possessiveness. And want. So much want. He wanted to taste the boy, to touch him, to get inside of him. To own him.

Tristan suddenly muttered, sounding embarrassed, "If you mention this to anyone—"

"What did I tell you about unnecessary threats?" Zach pressed his nose behind Tristan's ear and inhaled deeply. Tristan's scent was doing things to him, all of them uncomfortable for various reasons. "You don't have to threaten me. I know: you're mean, heartless, and tough."

"I am," Tristan said defensively, though he showed no inclination to remove himself from Zach's arms. "Don't make fun of me." He peeked over Zach's shoulder. "Nick is looking at us. Let go of me before he gets any ideas."

Zach tried to, but his body didn't obey any signals from his brain. It felt like his arms weighed a ton; they refused to move. The image of his brother touching Tristan earlier flashed through his mind, and his gut shriveled into a hard, icy ball. His arms tightened.

"Zach?" Tristan said.

Zach turned his head and threw over his shoulder, "Go inside."

"Glad to see I'm not the only one you order around," Tristan said with a smile in his voice.

"Is he gone?" Zach asked, sliding his hands down to rest on Tristan's lower back, just above the curve of his ass.

It felt like the most natural thing in the world. His hands fit perfectly there. Tristan fit perfectly in his arms.

"Uh huh," Tristan said, practically melting into him. "Zach?"

"Mmm?"

"You're still in an open relationship, right?"

Zach sucked a breath in. "Yes."

A long silence followed.

Tristan extracted himself from Zach's arms and stepped back. His cheekbones were a little flushed, but other than that he looked like his normal self again. He no longer seemed so agitated. Zach still wanted to know what had upset him.

Tristan rubbed a hand behind his neck. "Then, come over tonight. Just tonight. If you want." He bit his lip and averted his eyes, already looking like he regretted saying that. "All right, bye." He strode to his car briskly and got in. The engine roared and he was off.

Zach stood still after the car was long gone.

Come over tonight. Just tonight. If you want.

The words resonated through his body, sending waves of almost painful need through him. The temptation was beyond anything he had ever experienced.

Shaking his head, Zach headed back inside.

When he entered the house, Zach came to a halt as four pairs of eyes looked at him.

"So, what was that about?" Ryan asked. "That wasn't how I imagined him."

"It's none of our business," James said.

"Actually, I disagree," Ryan said. "He bolted out when we came, so I sort of take it personally."

"James is right," Zach said. "It's none of your business, Ryan."

"But it's yours?" Nick cut in.

Was that jealousy in Nick's voice? Fuck, what a mess.

Zach loved his brother—all of his brothers—but this was something he had to nip in the bud.

"Not yours," Zach said, staring Nick down, which was no longer as easy as it used to be now that they were almost the same height. Nick was no longer the kid who had worshiped him and followed him around like a puppy—he was a man—and Zach didn't delude himself into thinking that right now Nick saw him as his eldest brother. Nick stepped closer.

"Whoa, what the hell?" Ryan said, jumping between them. "What's going on?"

"Zach, a word," Donna said suddenly.

Zach looked away from Nick only after Nick dropped his gaze.

"Zach," Donna said again.

Reluctantly, he followed her into the kitchen and closed the door.

She crossed her arms over her chest and regarded him calmly for a moment before saying, "You lied."

He frowned. "What?"

"You said it was just lust and that you could control it. When he got upset, you didn't behave like a man in lust, Zach. You behaved like a concerned boyfriend."

Zach averted his eyes. "I didn't."

"Really? You should have seen your face when you told Nick to stay put. It was clear you thought you had the right to deal with the situation even though he was Nick's date."

"He wasn't Nick's date," Zach said testily.

Donna chuckled. "See? You hate even the suggestion that he was someone else's."

When he remained silent, a humorless smile appeared on her face. "You know, I always thought you were like me: that you were too practical and rational to feel silly emotions like jealousy. But apparently, it just took the right person to wake up your primitive side."

Zach couldn't even form the words of denial that rose up in his throat. He thought about what it probably looked like. He did behave like a jealous man around Tristan. Because he was jealous. He was. There was no point denying it.

"Where are you going with this?" he said quietly.

She bit her lip. "I want my husband to be devoted to me. I don't mean sex—you know I don't care much about it as long as we have an understanding. I mean emotional commitment. Can you honestly say that if we get married, you will not drool, pine and get jealous over your brother's boyfriend?"

"If?" Zach said.

She shrugged. "If—when—I don't know. After what I've seen, I'm not sure this is what you want—what *I* want."

Zach stared at her. "We've been together for ten years. We're getting married in a month. The invitations have been sent out. I'm not leaving you at the altar."

"I know you won't," she said. "You're too responsible for that. But that's not enough. I need more."

"I know you, Donna," Zach said, stepping closer to her and touching her cheek. He wasn't fooled by her calm tone. No matter what she said, he knew she would be very hurt and embarrassed if he broke the engagement so close to the wedding. "It would be mortifying for you if we canceled the wedding now."

"I prefer to be mortified for a few days to marrying a man who's crazy about someone else."

Zach averted his gaze again. "I'm not—"

"Stop," she said, putting a hand to his lips. "Stop and think. I'll give you a week to figure it out. When—if—we marry, I want it to be for the right reasons, not because you feel responsible and guilty and all that bullshit. I deserve better. And you do, too. So figure out what—and who— you really want to be with. I hope it's me, but if it's not, it won't be the end of the world for me. I'm a self-sufficient woman and I don't need a man to be happy." She smiled without much mirth. "I'm not going to lie to you: I'm not saying I'm not mad or upset—I am—I'm mad as hell—but I won't be mad at you forever, in any case. Just don't lie to me or to yourself. We'd been friends long before we became lovers and nothing will change that."

He kissed her on the temple. "You're amazing, you know that, right?"

"I know," she said, her tone very light. "I'm the best thing that ever happened to you. You'd better remember that."

As he watched her go, he wished he could erase the last few months and convince her that she was the one he wanted to be with.

He couldn't do it now. He had to convince himself first.

Come over tonight. Just tonight. If you want.

Zach closed his eyes.

Chapter 23

He hadn't come. Of course he hadn't.

Tristan stared at the shadows dancing on his far wall. The tight feeling in his chest was just mortification. It was. Except he'd never been all that good at lying to himself. He knew what this feeling was and *that* knowledge made him mortified.

Tristan rolled over, punched his pillow a few times, and kicked off his sheets. He squeezed his eyes shut. He had a game tomorrow, his first game in months. He had to sleep. He had to forget what a fool he'd made of himself and sleep. But just as he'd expected, sleep wouldn't come.

It took a long time, but eventually, he succumbed to his emotional exhaustion and drifted off.

He dreamed of Zach's lips kissing his neck. Of his stubble scratching his skin. Zach's lips were gentle. Almost reverent. They dragged up Tristan's neck to his ear and bit gently. "You should have made me give the goddamn key back."

Tristan's eyes flew open. He wasn't dreaming. He could feel Zach's warm breath on his ear. Could smell him.

Shivering, Tristan turned onto his back and tried to make out Zach's face in the darkness. He couldn't.

Silence fell upon the dark room, their uneven breathing the only sound that could be heard, and Tristan was literally trembling. He wanted to reach out and touch.

Badly.

"Tristan." Zach released a somewhat shaky sigh, letting his body drop on top of him.

Tristan let out a soft moan. If he were honest, he missed this as much as the sex: the sensation of Zach's body, heavy and *perfect* on him, cutting him off from the rest of the world and making it hard to focus on anything but him. The weight was a bit too much and it was hard to breathe, and it was just perfect. Before he knew what he was doing, Tristan had his legs wrapped around Zach.

Zach dropped his face into the crook of Tristan's neck. Took a deep breath. "You're naked," he ground out. "Why are you naked, damn you?"

"Why aren't you?" Tristan whispered, closing his eyes as Zach sucked a bruise into his neck.

"I'm not here for this," Zach said, giving him another hickey.

Ignoring his words, Tristan tugged Zach's shirt off and ran his hands over the expanse of Zach's wide back. "I want you. Want you inside me."

Zach drew in a ragged breath. "I'm not here for this," he tried again, sounding even more unconvincing. "We need to talk."

Tristan didn't want to talk. He knew what Zach was going to say. He didn't need to hear it. He was just a dirty little secret, something shameful, something to have in the darkness before Zach rode off into the sunset with his bride.

Zach was here because he couldn't help himself—not because he *wanted* to be here. If Zach had truly wanted to be here, he wouldn't resist coming until it was the middle of the night. Tristan had no delusions. He was good enough for a fuck, but he wasn't good enough for…for anything else.

"Come on," he murmured, rolling his hips a little and running his fingers through Zach's hair. "I know you want to. You can have me. One more time."

A growl tore out of Zach's throat and then Zach was kissing him and Tristan was kissing back, both of them moaning, greedy and desperate. He missed this, he missed this, God, he missed this and missed him. So fucking much.

"Your mouth should be fucking outlawed," Zach rasped, sucking and nibbling on Tristan's bottom lip.

Tristan didn't say anything; he couldn't. His mind felt like cotton, all his senses focused on his mouth—and Zach's mouth—all he could do was soak up Zach's kisses and touches. He barely noticed Zach's undressing, but he definitely noticed when their naked bodies pressed together tightly, skin to skin. He moaned as Zach's parted lips dragged deliciously across his chest, closed on his nipple and *sucked*. When Zach released his nipple from his mouth with a pop and charted a path with his lips down to Tristan's belly button, Tristan groaned and shoved Zach's head lower.

Zach bypassed his aching cock, trailing his tongue between Tristan's thighs. Lifting Tristan's hips, Zach started licking his hole, quickly reducing Tristan to a quivering, moaning mess. Panting, Tristan pushed back against the tongue, needing more. Zach gripped his hip tighter and plunged his tongue deeper, emitting a groan that vibrated against the tender flesh.

God. God. Tristan couldn't think, racked by the shudders rolling through his body at each swipe of Zach's tongue. His thighs were trembling, his back was arching, and the roaring rush of pleasure pounding through his veins was the only thing he could hear for a very long time. He could barely register Zach prepping and stretching him hurriedly—so far gone he was. He just wanted.

When Zach took his fingers and tongue away, Tristan whined. He moved his hips and dug his fingers into Zach's muscular buttocks. A moan ripped out of his throat as Zach's cock dragged deliciously against the rim of his hole. "Zach, come on."

"Yeah—just give me a—" Zach said and pushed inside of him, his strong hands stroking Tristan's thighs and keeping them wide apart. Zach moved very slowly, his body shuddering above him and tense as hell. "Okay?" he said when he bottomed out.

Tristan stared at the dark ceiling, his eyes watering. "Perfect." He immediately regretted saying it, but it still sounded less cringe-worthy than his needy thoughts.

Zach started moving and Tristan closed his eyes. His head collapsed back against the pillow, his back arching off the bed as Zach quickly picked up speed, Zach's hand spreading over his side and the other running down his leg. Tristan couldn't help but just let it out—string a whole slur of half-words and curses together as Zach snapped his hips into him at an intensity that showed just how fucking badly he wanted this, too.

He wasn't going to last. He pulled Zach tighter to him, heat racing through his veins, the flames licking over his flesh, and the ache building with each thrust of Zach's cock, filling him up so perfectly, as if it was made for him, which was all kinds of ridiculous.

But right now, just for a little while, Zach's cock was his, *Zach* was his, only his, his, his, *his*—

He came with a pained moan that was so loud he surprised himself, his fingernails digging into Zach's back as his body tensed with waves of pleasure that swept through him, like nothing he'd ever felt.

Zach didn't stop moving, his thrusts becoming rougher, his fingers gripping Tristan's thighs hard, harder—

"Yeah, that's it," Zach muttered, sounding absolutely wrecked. "You feel so good, so perfect, wanna come in you—" He shuddered and came with a stifled groan, and Tristan's face contorted as Zach pumped into him, reveling in it way too much, that it was Zach's seed filling him, hot and creamy, into his deepest places. God, this was fucked up.

When Zach started kissing his face softly, kissing him everywhere, Tristan couldn't fucking deal with it anymore. He just couldn't.

He didn't trust his voice not to break. This hadn't been a good day for him and he felt…fragile. Weak and pathetic and needier than ever.

"Tristan?" The note of concern in Zach's voice reminded him of the way Zach had held him and comforted him earlier that evening. Suddenly, a rush of pure hatred burned through him. Why had Zach done it? Why was he here at all? Why was Zach kissing him like that? Like he cared. Like Tristan meant something to him. Something precious.

"Go," Tristan said roughly. "You should go."

A few seconds passed in silence.

Zach reached out to the bedside lamp.

"Don't," Tristan bit off.

He didn't want the light. He trusted his face even less than he trusted his voice. Darkness was perfect for this. He didn't want to see Zach. Didn't want Zach to see him until he'd managed to compose himself.

"Get out," Tristan whispered.

He could feel Zach's eyes on him. "Get out? Do you mean—?"

"You know what I mean," Tristan said. *Get out of my life.*

Silence.

At last, Zach pulled out and rolled off him.

Tristan swallowed, feeling hollow in more ways than one. He pulled the sheets to his chin and stared unseeingly into the darkness, fighting the impulse to say something scathing and hurtful. Zach knew him and would see right through it. They were going separate ways in life and would likely never see each other again, but it didn't mean Tristan wanted Zach to remember him as that pathetic kid who got a little too attached after a month of sex.

The rustling of clothes stopped, and an odd heaviness settled in Tristan's chest.

The silence stretched out, becoming unbearable.

Tristan closed his eyes and whispered again, "Get out." *Before I make a fool of myself and beg you to dump your fiancée for me.*

He felt more than heard Zach leave.

When Tristan switched on the bedside lamp, the first thing he saw was the key on the nightstand.

The shiny metal glinted in the dim light.

He curled his fingers around it before throwing it across the room.

Something shattered and broke and he remembered what Lydia had told him a while back.

I hope one day you'll fall in love. And that person will bring you to your knees.

A ripping, unsteady laugh tore out of him. He laughed and laughed and laughed until there was nothing left in him.

Chapter 24

The house was dark and quiet when Zach let himself in. He locked the door, turned on the light, and went directly to the mini-bar. He grabbed a bottle of whiskey and took a swig.

"Drinking alone at night?"

Zach stiffened at the sound of Nick's voice. "It's late," he said curtly. "Go to sleep."

"I'm a little too old to have a bedtime."

Zach took a gulp of whiskey. "It's three in the morning, I'm knackered, and not in a good mood, Nick."

"I can see that," Nick said, his tone as dry. "You haven't been in a good mood the entire evening. Ever since—"

"Where are Ryan and James?" Zach said. When he'd left the house a little after midnight, they had still been there.

"Very subtle," Nick said. "But in case you really care, they're upstairs, sleeping like babies—oddly enough, not together. So, about—"

Zach walked out of the room.

But Nick, being Nick, didn't get the hint and followed him out to the terrace.

Ignoring him, Zach gulped his whiskey and stretched himself out in the chaise lounge. He closed his eyes and focused on the sound of the wind blowing through the trees.

"You know, at first I was pissed off," Nick said. "Of course I was pissed off. Don't remember the last time my ego has taken a beating like that. It kind of sucks when the hot guy I've been hitting on the entire evening tells me to fuck off and then becomes all touchy-feely with my brother."

Zach opened his eyes. "Forget about him," he said flatly.

Nick lit a cigarette. "If I didn't know better, I'd think you have some personal interest." He took a drag and exhaled. "You know, some people say homosexuality is genetic. I used to think they were wrong—I mean, I thought I was the only one in the family—but maybe they're onto something. Though, who knows, maybe you *are* straight." He chuckled. "He sure is hot enough to tempt a monk. Though, it looks like he has one hell of an attitude lurking behind his pretty face, but it's kind of hot. The craziest, bitchy ones are often fantastic in the sack. He's probably like a wild cat, all hisses and claws—"

Zach gritted his teeth. "You'll never find out, so stop bloody talking about it."

He could feel Nick's curious gaze on him.

"I've never seen you get so riled up when other men hit on Donna," Nick said, taking another drag from his cigarette. "I know you've been together forever, but to be honest, sometimes I thought you couldn't be that into her if she doesn't make your blood turn hot.

"I mean, I'm all for open relationships, but…" He snorted a laugh. "We're still cavemen at heart when it comes to our shit. It's a biological instinct."

"Nick," Zach said evenly. "Go to bed."

Nick sighed. "I hate when you use that voice on me. Fine, I'll leave you to your brooding." Nick moved to the door but paused. "I can't say I felt very brotherly this evening, but…you're my brother." His voice got gruff and a little awkward. "I love you and I've always looked up to you, you know that. You've always done the right thing by us. But sometimes doing the right thing won't make you happy. Don't make a mistake. Do what feels right for once, not what you think is right." Nick stubbed out his cigarette and went inside.

Zach stared at the murky sky. Do what feels right?

He thought of Donna's confident smile, the way she fit into his family seamlessly, the way everything was easy and effortless with her. Donna was his friend of twenty years. She had been a part of his life for so long that he couldn't imagine it without her.

Then his thoughts turned to the lovely blue-green eyes and scowling mouth, and a rush of frustration and gut-twisting longing swept through him. Nothing was easy and effortless with Tristan. To say Tristan had issues was to say nothing. There was also the matter of Tristan being a celebrity in the closet, which presented a whole different set of problems.

By all counts, Donna was the right choice and Tristan was the wrong choice.

And he wasn't even sure whether Tristan was a choice at all. He didn't know what Tristan wanted from him—if he even wanted anything. Tristan had certainly made it clear that he wanted Zach out of his life.

Zach bit the inside of his cheek hard as he remembered Tristan's voice when he told Zach to get out. He could hear anger and hatred in Tristan's voice. But he could also hear the fear, hurt and vulnerability, and that had almost been Zach's undoing. He had wanted to kiss all the hurt away, ready to do anything to make it better—and that freaked him out enough to leave.

Fuck, he was worse than all those people Tristan had eating out of his hand. They didn't know the real Tristan; *he* had no such excuse. The mere fact that he was even considering leaving his long-time girlfriend practically at the altar for the guy who gave him no indication that his feelings were reciprocated was pure madness. If Tristan had given him a hint that he wanted them to be more than fuck-buddies, it would have been easier.

Zach gave a harsh chuckle.

Who was he kidding? If he had known for sure that Tristan had feelings for him, there would be no choice at all. If he was this unreasonable and besotted while Tristan kept him at an arm's length, he had no delusions what would happen if Tristan admitted that he wanted to be his.

His.

A wave of longing rolled through him and Zach cursed through his teeth. Christ. When had this thing become so fucking deep?

This thing? Tristan voice teased him in his head. *Stop being such a coward. Put a name to it.*

Zach closed his eyes, trying to ignore the voice, to no avail.

I prefer to be mortified for a few days to marrying a man who's crazy about someone else. When—if—we marry, I want it to be for the right reasons, not because you feel responsible and guilty and all that bullshit. Figure out who you want, Zach.

Zach downed the rest of the whiskey.
It was going to be a long night.

Chapter 25

"You look like shit," Ryan said, looking up from the sandwich he was making. "Rough night?"

Zach opened the fridge and poured himself a glass of orange juice. He downed it in one go, sat at the table, and dropped his pounding head into his hands.

"I take it as a yes," Ryan said with a laugh, putting a cup of coffee in front of him. "How many times do we have to have this conversation? You're poisoning your body."

Sometimes Zach really hated his brothers. They all had become cheeky as hell.

"Ryan," Zach ground out. "Shut up."

A laugh came from the doorway, making him wince.

"I absolutely love the little boy look you get whenever Zach uses that voice," James said, walking into the room and dropping into the chair beside to Ryan. He grabbed the sandwich Ryan had made and started eating.

"That was mine," Ryan said.

"Yeah and so?" James said with an arrogant look.

Rolling his eyes, Ryan started making himself another. "You aren't your dad, you can't pull it off. You just look like a tool. As always."

James gave him a half-hearted punch on the chest. Ryan laughed and tugged him into a playful headlock.

"Get out of my house, kids," Zach said, rubbing his temples. "Your cheerfulness is nauseating."

"You know you love us," James said with a grin, Ryan's arm still around his neck.

Zach blinked blearily and did a double take. Why hadn't he noticed before that James's eyes were just like Tristan's?

But then again, he usually didn't have the habit of noticing men's eyes.

Because of James's pale complexion and hair, the effect wasn't as striking, and James's eyes were unguarded, but they were exactly like Tristan's: a unique, distinct color and slightly exotic shape. Of course it could be a coincidence, but coupled with Tristan's mini-breakdown after Ryan and James's arrival...

His forehead creasing, Zach thought of what little he knew of Tristan's family. It was common knowledge that Tristan came from a poor background and that his mother died when he was five or six. His father...

Zach frowned as he remembered what Tristan had told him about his father. He was married—and very possibly had kids. He was also an earl.

An earl.

Zach stared at James.

The kid's father was an earl, too, which was usually an endless source of jokes for Ryan. Although it seemed unlikely that James's top-lofty father could have something in common with Tristan's mother, stranger things happened, especially if Tristan had inherited his exquisite looks from his mother. There weren't that many rich, high-handed earls in England anymore.

"Do you look like your dad?" Zach asked. Although he had seen the Earl of Lytton a few times on the TV—he was a pretty prominent politician—Zach certainly hadn't paid attention to the man's eyes. All he remembered was confidence bordering on arrogance.

James gave him a startled look. "What? No, not really. Well, my eyes are just like his, but all Grayson men have the Grayson eyes, so it doesn't really count." He chuckled. "My dad says it's because the Grayson bloodline is so superior, the Grayson eyes always breed true."

Grinning, Ryan said, "Your eyes remind me of the tiling in the swimming pool locker rooms."

James elbowed him. "At least mine aren't the color of a toad."

"You're just jealous your eyes aren't half as pretty as mine."

"Yeah, sure."

Zach tuned them out, staring at his cup. Tristan knew he was the Earl of Lytton's son. Judging by his reaction, he knew James was his brother, the son his father hadn't rejected. The son who had all the privileges and a loving family as he grew up.

Zach shifted his gaze back to James. He watched him grin and laugh with Ryan, so carefree and happy.

James had countless friends. He had been an unofficial member of the Hardaway family ever since he and Ryan had become friends as kids. James had loving parents who doted on him every moment and gave him everything he wanted. James was a goddamn viscount.

Zach thought of the boy who never had any of that. Who had been rejected by a parent when he needed him the most. Who didn't know how to connect to people. Who didn't have a single person he could truly call a friend.

Who pretended to be something he wasn't just to be liked. Who didn't know how to express any positive emotion. Who never knew love—and likely didn't know how to ask for it.

Who would never ask for it.

Shit.

Zach's lips thinned. So many things made so much sense now. He had sometimes suspected that Tristan actually had low self-esteem, but until now he hadn't realized the extent of it. Deep down, Tristan would always expect to be rejected in favor of someone else, no matter how confident and arrogant he might seem. Behind all the walls he'd put up, the boy did have very low self-esteem. Tristan would never confess his feelings first—if he did have them.

Now the question was:

Was he willing to break his engagement for such an uncertain thing?

Zach stood and left the kitchen. He fished his phone out of his pocket, found the contact he wanted, and pressed Call.

"We need to talk," he said.

Chapter 26

Tristan stood at the center of the pitch, waiting for the game to start. He looked around, taking it all in: the noise of the crowd, the familiar look of determination on his teammates' faces, flashes of cameras everywhere. He tried to build up the excitement he used to feel, but it was futile when he felt like death warmed over. His eyes still felt like sandpaper after the sleepless night, and he could feel the nauseous tide of a rising headache at his temples.

The cheering from the crowd resonated through his tired body. It took him a moment to realize they were chanting his name. His strained smile turned genuine and Tristan applauded, thanking the fans and causing another wave of "TRISTAN, TRISTAN, TRISTAN."

At last, the whistle was blown and the match started.

For a while, everything was fine. His groin didn't bother him at all, and his headache receded, letting him enjoy the game.

Nothing prepared him for what happened twenty minutes into the game.

Later, everyone would say it was just a matter of being in the wrong place at the wrong time.

Footballers got their legs kicked at least a couple of times every match; it was nothing unusual or particularly dangerous. But when Tristan rushed forward after his team won a corner and two players tackled him, a pain like no other shot through his left leg, making him nearly black out as the leg gave out.

He breathed through pain and dizziness and focused his eyes on his leg. Bile rose to his throat when he saw that the bone pierced the skin and his leg was bent unnaturally below the knee in several places. There was blood. Lots and lots of blood. So much blood.

He was only vaguely aware of the other players shouting and the medics rushing to his side. He saw Jared's grim face, but he didn't need to look at Jared's face to know that this was bad. He'd been injured before many times, but never like this.

His eyes wet from pain, Tristan looked at the sky as he was carried off the pitch on a stretcher.

The fans applauded him.

Tristan squeezed his eyes shut. Somewhere deep in his gut, he knew they were applauding him for the last time. He couldn't even say he was surprised. Good things never lasted. Not for him.

He was almost glad when the pain became too much and he passed out.

When he opened his eyes next time, he was in a pristine hospital room and he had a cast on his left leg. The absence of pain surprised him before he realized that he was probably on painkillers.

"How do you feel?"

Tristan turned his head and found Jared standing there.

"Just tell me how bad it is."

Jared glanced at Gabriel, who was hovering by the door, before looking at Tristan again.

"You have a multiple compound fracture of both the tibia and fibula in your left leg. We performed a surgery, but…"

"But I'm never going to recover," Tristan said.

"You will," Jared said firmly. "You will get full function of your leg back. Just…"

"My career is over."

A lengthy silence fell.

Tristan almost laughed. It was kind of hilarious that he'd spent the last few months getting fit for the World Cup only to get a career-ending injury in the first game after his recovery.

"There's a chance you will be able to play again," Jared said.

Tristan smiled.

"Sure there is. But even if I do, I'll never be as good as I used to be. Right?"

Jared pursed his lips briefly. "Saying never isn't a good idea. Every case is different. I've known a player who was able to return after a year of intense physical therapy and he didn't experience any problems. But in your case…it's difficult to say.

"Your leg was broken in multiples places, and the injury is extremely unstable because of many bone fragments and large degrees of displacement. There's a lot of damage to the surrounding muscles, tendons, and ligaments.

"You'll be able to walk again soon enough, but it's difficult to say how well the leg will heal. Playing football professionally after such an injury would always be a risk, no matter how well you recover."

"Yeah," Tristan said. "Even if I recover, I'll be damaged goods. My contract with Chelsea is ending. Who would want such an injury-prone player? I had three groin injuries in half a year and now I got a career-threatening injury in the first game after my recovery and will be out for at least a year. No top club would take a risk on me. I'd never agree to play for a mid-table club."

He could see that Jared privately agreed with him, but aloud Jared said, "In any case, it's not something you have to worry about now. You need to rest. Gabe, let's go."

"Give me a minute," Gabriel said, touching Jared's wrist.

Jared shot him a stern look. "Don't upset my patient."

Gabriel smiled a little. "No promises. Go."

Closing the door after Jared, Gabriel turned around and looked at Tristan.

"Yeah, you can gloat now," Tristan said tiredly, closing his eyes. "I'm sure you think it's nothing I don't deserve."

"I wish I could gloat. I'm sure you would if our places were reversed."

Tristan chuckled. "Are you saying you actually give a shit about me? I'm touched, Gabe."

"Ugh!" Gabriel let out a frustrated noise. "Why are you always so difficult?"

"Bugger off and stop bothering me. Don't you see I'm busy?"

"Fine. I'll leave you to your self-pity."

Tristan opened his eyes and glared at him. "All right. Talk."

"Stop being such a quitter," Gabriel said quietly, a small furrow between his brows.

"Yeah, it sucks, but it could have been worse, Tristan. Like, you could have damaged your spine and could have been paralyzed. Trust me, it sucks much more. When I got injured, the doctors said I could never walk again, much less play football. But I never gave up and here I am."

"Yeah, you're stronger and better than me. Nothing new here. Now get the hell out of here." To his utter mortification, his voice got suspiciously thick, and Tristan glared harder at his adoptive brother.

Pursing his lips, Gabriel left, muttering something under his breath.

When the door shut behind him, Tristan closed his eyes again.

It was easy for Gabe to say. When Gabe had been injured, he had Jared to hold his hand and hug it better. Tristan had no one. Not that he needed anyone.

Tristan buried his face in the pillow. It smelled of hospital disinfectant.

If his eyes were wet, well, his leg was broken to pieces and his career was over. It was as good excuse as any.

Chapter 27

The problem with visiting football stars in hospitals was the fact that it was pretty much impossible. He was no longer Tristan's physiotherapist, nor was he a relative.

Zach glanced around the hospital lobby and tried Jared's number again, and again got his voice mail.

"Zach?"

He looked up, relief coursing through him when he saw Gabriel. "How is he?"

Gabriel gave him a strange look. "You're here because of Tristan?"

Was it so hard to believe?

"Yes," Zach said, a little harder than he had intended. He wasn't sure how much Gabe knew, anyway. "Is he okay?"

Gabriel pulled a face. "He's as bitchy and difficult as usual. But...well, you've probably seen the injury, yeah?"

Zach nodded jerkily. Of course he had.

He hadn't seen it live on TV—he had been leaving Donna's place at the time—but he looked it up after Nick had called him, sounding freaked out.

"It looked gruesome," he said roughly. As a physiotherapist, he'd seen some terrible injuries, but seeing Tristan's leg broken in multiple places, with bones sticking out and blood everywhere, made him ill and helplessly furious.

"It looked worse in person," Gabriel said, grimacing. "A couple of our players actually threw up. I've seen broken legs before, but this is something else. The FA disqualified those morons."

"Good." Zach took a deep breath and unclenched his fist. "How is he?"

Gabriel shrugged. "Jared says the surgery went well, but Tristan will need extensive physiotherapy. He'll walk again soon enough, but as far as his professional career goes..." He shrugged again.

Zach couldn't say he was surprised. As soon as he had seen the extent of Tristan's injury, he knew the implications of it. "I want to see him. Can you get me in?"

Cocking his head to the side, Gabriel studied him. "Why? I think he's upset enough."

"Not to be rude, Gabe, but since when do you give a shit about him?"

"I don't," Gabriel said immediately, flushing. "I really don't."

Zach shook his head. The DuVal brothers had the strangest relationship. "You both have issues."

Gabriel gave him a lopsided smile. "I'm not gonna argue with that. But at least I'm not emotionally constipated like him."

Zach wasn't going to argue with *that*. "I've got to talk to him, Gabe."

"Not sure talking to him now is a good idea. He told me to leave him alone."

"No offense, but I'm not you."

"There's that." Gabriel crossed his arms over his chest. "But what do you want with him?"

Zach almost smiled. For all of Gabe's claims that he didn't care about his brother at all, he gave the opposite impression. "I'll tell Tristan what I want with him. After you get me inside."

Gabriel eyed him for a moment before nodding and motioning him to follow him. "Let's go."

On the VIP floor, Gabriel came to a halt in front of a door and turned to Zach. "If you make me regret it, you will—"

"You're cute when you try threatening people like Tristan does," Zach said with a smile before dropping it and looking Gabriel in the eye. "Maybe you should actually tell him you care. You're the closest thing he has to a family."

Gabe made a face and said reluctantly, "I'll think about it."

Opening the door, Zach entered the room and shut it quietly.

His eyes zeroed in on the figure on the bed. His gaze skimmed over the cast on Tristan's leg before stopping on Tristan's nape. Tristan had his face buried in the pillow, his fingers clenching the pillow so hard his knuckles were white. The knot of worry that had taken up permanent residence in Zach's stomach since he'd found out about the injury coiled tighter as a wave of possessive protectiveness surged through him.

Zach quietly walked to the bed and stared at the back of Tristan's head. Despite his words to Gabe, he wasn't all that sure that Tristan would want to see him. He'd made a lot of assumptions about Tristan.

He couldn't know for sure that he hadn't imagined what wasn't there. As much as it pained him to admit it, he couldn't trust himself when it came to Tristan: He was unreasonable around him, behaving like a man possessed, just wanting to *have* him in every possible way.

The truth was, he wanted Tristan to want him. He wanted Tristan to need him. There was nothing rational or practical about it. Tristan was trouble. Tristan was a complication he didn't need in his life. And yet, he wanted the brat in his arms, all *his* for bitching at, kissing, scolding, fucking and adoring, with all his prickly attitude. It was irrational as hell. And that was why he couldn't trust himself to interpret Tristan's feelings correctly.

Zach lifted his hand and brushed a long, dark eyelash off Tristan's cheek. It was moist.

Flinching, Tristan turned his head and stared at him unblinkingly. His nose was red, his lips were chapped, and his eyes were red and wet. There was nothing pretty about him right now. Zach wanted to kiss him.

So he did.

He leaned down and fit their lips together. A soft, little whine escaped Tristan's mouth. Burying his fingers in Tristan's hair, Zach kissed him deeper, sucking and biting on those plush lips. Sweet mercy. He couldn't get enough of this mouth. Tristan's hands looped around his neck, raked through his hair and tugged him closer, those little sighs and moans going straight to Zach's cock—and his heart. Christ, how the hell had he gotten in so deep, so quick?

Suddenly, Tristan tore his mouth away and glared at him. "What do you think you're doing?"

"Kissing you," Zach said, kissing one corner of his mouth and then the other one.

Tristan's lips parted before he smacked Zach on the head and pushed him away. "Stop that!" Tristan's brows drew together suspiciously. "Why are you here?" His eyes narrowed. "Are you feeling *sorry* for me?"

Zach laughed. "God forbid. Who in their right mind would feel sorry for you?"

The suspicious look didn't vanish from Tristan's face, though his shoulders relaxed a little. "Then why are you here?"

Zach took a seat on the bed. "Am I not allowed to be worried for my former patient? Your getting injured in your first game doesn't exactly put me in a good light." He had meant it as a joke, but he instantly regretted it when Tristan dropped his gaze. Zach stroked the inside of Tristan's wrist until Tristan lifted his eyes again. "I wanted to make sure you were okay," Zach said roughly.

Tristan smiled. The smile didn't quite reach his eyes. "I'll never play football again. But otherwise I'm just peachy. You can go now." He pulled his hand away from Zach's and curled it by his side.

"You can play again—"

"Don't," Tristan said. "I don't want comforting lies. Not from you."

Zach looked at the cast.

"I won't lie to you," he said. "I've had patients with less severe broken leg injuries than yours who couldn't successfully return to professional sports. I've had patients who made successful comebacks and were as good as new." He looked Tristan in the eye. "But you can play football again for sure. Even if not professionally, you can—"

"If I can't play professionally, there's no point," Tristan said, his eyes glistening.

He smiled. "You called me narcissistic once and you were right. The fans are important to me. When they sing my name, urging me forward, it's—it feels so…special. I feel…" He trailed off, a wistful look on his face.

"Loved?" Zach said quietly.

Tristan's jaw clenched.

"You loved feeling loved," Zach said. That wasn't a question, and with every moment that Tristan didn't deny it, Zach was more and more certain that he was right. "That's why you think you have to play professionally to feel it again."

Tristan averted his gaze.

Taking Tristan's chin with his fingers, Zach tipped his face up, forcing him to meet his eye. "You won't need football for that."

Tristan looked at him unblinkingly, as if he didn't understand what Zach was talking about.

At last, his eyes widened. He flushed, scowled, then looked away before darting a glance at Zach again. If it had been someone else, Zach would have thought Tristan was shy.

Tristan gave him a scathing look. "Where's your fiancée?"

"I don't have a fiancée," Zach said. "Not anymore."

Tristan seemed to stop breathing. He just stared.

"Why?" he said at last.

"We talked," Zach said curtly.

The conversation had been the hardest in his life. He knew he and Donna would be okay eventually—they'd been friends far longer than lovers, and their friendship couldn't be destroyed easily—but right now he wasn't exactly Donna's favorite person in the world.

"We decided it would be pointless to marry if I want to be with someone else. She deserves better. We both do."

Tristan was blinking rapidly, looking anywhere but at him. "Just like that?" Before Zach could say anything, Tristan shot him a hostile look. "Why are you telling me this? What does it have to do with me?"

Zach felt a rush of overwhelming affection mixed with sadness. No one should be so guarded at Tristan's age.

"You know," he said gently. Holding Tristan's gaze, Zach put his hand next to Tristan's, palm up.

Tristan eyed the hand as though it was a poisonous snake. "I—I don't understand."

"You do. Come on." Zach smiled. "Where's my confident, arrogant brat?"

Slowly, very slowly, Tristan moved his hand until their fingers curled together.

Tristan's scowl deepened. "I'll kill you if this is a joke," he grumbled, his voice a little unsteady.

Zach chuckled. "This must really be love, because there's no other reason for me to find your constant bitching adorable."

Tristan glowered at him, and Zach finally gave in to the urge to kiss that scowling mouth again.

Minutes later, when they pulled apart, Tristan had a soft, thoroughly kissed look on his face. He was so bloody lovely that Zach just had to kiss him again.

And again.

Fuck, this was ridiculous.

"Wait," Tristan said suddenly, panting a little. "Are you really saying that you, like, love me?" He tripped a little on the word "love" and looked at Zach with suspicion.

Christ.

Zach brushed Tristan's flushed cheek with his thumb. "You're such a little shit," he murmured, trailing kisses on Tristan's jawline. "You drive me crazy in a good way and in a bad way. But yeah, I'm pretty sure I love you. I have no idea how that happened, but I do."

Tristan's hand squeezed his hand almost painfully. He buried his face in Zach's shoulder and muttered a few words.

Zach's heart somersaulted into his throat. "What was that?" he said wryly, even though he had heard him perfectly.

Tristan punched him in the shoulder. "I said I hate you."

Zach hid his smile in Tristan's hair and breathed in deeply. God. He hoped these feelings would get a little less intense with time. Feeling so much was just wrong for a rational thirty-year-old man.

"I hate you, too," Zach said, wrapping his arms around Tristan. He thought back to their first meeting. If someone back then had told him he would become so utterly besotted with that boy within the next few months, he would have thought they were crazy.

Tristan sighed, slipping his arms around Zach, too. "You'll never get rid of me."

"I'm oddly okay with that."

Tristan dug his fingers into his back. "And I'm not Donna. No open relationship bullshit. I don't share."

"Neither do I. Not you." Zach nuzzled the spot behind Tristan's ear. He bit Tristan's earlobe. "If you flirt with Nick again, I won't be responsible for the consequences."

Tristan pulled back a little and smirked, looking at him from under his eyelashes.

"Oh yeah? What are you gonna do to me?"

Zach's pulse skyrocketed. His prick twitched. His hands twitched.

Tristan gave him an all-knowing look.

"You little—" Zach laughed. "As soon as I fix your leg, we'll see to it."

"I thought your services were booked months in advance or something," Tristan said, cocking his head. "Don't you have other very important patients?"

Tristan might be teasing, but Zach's tone was completely serious when he replied, "You are not my patient. You're mine and I'll take care of you."

Tristan's smirk disappeared and he simply looked at Zach for a long moment. Then, a small smile tugged at Tristan's lips before transforming into a bright, beautiful smile, his aquamarine eyes shining with warmth, and Zach's breath caught in his throat. Fuck. He had it so bad.

"You're beautiful," Zach said hoarsely. He wasn't talking about Tristan's looks.

Tristan stared at him wide-eyed before shaking his head a little.

"You are," Zach said. "It's all in the eyes."

Blushing and looking generally uncomfortable, Tristan shook his head again.

Zach chuckled. "Don't you argue with me. I'm always right."

Tristan rolled his eyes. "Prick. Not sure I want such a bossy prick as my physio again."

Zach gave him a short kiss, which turned into a very long one, because Jesus, that mouth drove him crazy.

When they finally parted for air, Zach stared. Tristan was flushed down to the collar of his hospital gown and his eyes were half-closed, pupils so wide there was only the smallest ring of blue. And that mouth, plump with blood and teeth marks, red and wet and swollen—Fucking hell. Get a grip, Hardaway.

Zach cleared his throat and smirked. "Who says you have a choice, dollface?"

Tristan's eyes narrowed and Zach had to kiss him again, because a pissed off Tristan was a sight to behold.

"Ugh, I hate you so much," Tristan said between kisses. "So much."

Zach laughed and kissed his nose. "You're adorable."

Tristan smacked him on the head.

Epilogue

Four months later

"Are you ever going to tell him you're his brother?"

Tristan glanced across the pool at Ryan and James before closing his eyes and burrowing deeper into Zach's side. The chaise lounge was too small for the two of them, but Tristan was perfectly okay with it. The sun was shining, the birds were chirping, and he had Zach's half-naked body against him: everything was right with the world. He wasn't in the mood to talk or think about James or James's father.

"Nope," he murmured, pressing his nose against Zach's arm. "Why should I? All we have in common is the guy who put his prick in our mothers and didn't use condoms."

Fingers started stroking his hair. Tristan leaned into the touch, a part of him still a bit surprised by how little he cared about being seen by other people. He used to break out in a cold sweat every time he imagined someone seeing him with another man. Now he didn't give a shit—one of the perks of being out of the spotlight. He was no longer a football star. Maybe he never would be again. Although Zach kept saying that his full recovery was likely, Tristan didn't really think he'd ever return to football.

His leg did feel better with every day, and most of the time his injury didn't trouble him much, but he didn't have the same confidence in his leg anymore. He doubted he ever would—at least not enough to play football professionally. And the thing was...he wasn't even sure he wanted to. Even thinking about pretending again to be something he wasn't and constantly hiding his relationship with Zach stressed Tristan out. It would be nearly impossible, anyway. Hiding a gay relationship was easier for Jared and Gabe, because they actually worked for the same football club and had work-related reasons to be seen together.

It didn't help that he pretty much lived with Zach nowadays. Tristan still wasn't sure how *that* had happened. He had never officially moved in, but rather migrated slowly: his toothbrush, his favorite pajamas, his tablet, one at a time. One day he just realized he had a lot of his shit in Zach's bedroom and hadn't returned to his own house in a week.

"Am I living with you?" Tristan had asked, staring at his favorite brand of coffee beans in Zach's kitchen.

Zach had just chuckled, brushed his lips against Tristan's neck and said, his voice still rough from sleep, "Morning."

It was nauseatingly domestic—and embarrassing. Tristan was glad he didn't have any friends to mock him. Gabriel was bad enough. The prick laughed every time he saw Tristan in Zach's house—which was far too often, since, unlike him, Zach did have friends and Jared and Gabe were among them.

"Maybe James would love to have a brother," Zach said, returning him to the present.

Tristan snorted. "He doesn't even like me."

"I can't imagine why," Zach said. "You're so nice to him."

Tristan opened his eyes and gave Zach an innocent look. "Hey, now that I don't have a personal assistant, I have to get my fun where I can."

Zach shook his head disapprovingly, but his eyes were amused and warm. Tristan suppressed a giddy smile. Ugh. He hated this thing.

"Anyway," Tristan said, trailing his fingers down Zach's chest lightly, until they rested just below the waistband of his trunks. "I wish he wasn't around so much. His stupid face annoys me."

"He's a good kid," Zach said. "And he and Ryan are pretty much a 2-in-1 package, so you'll have to suck it up."

Tristan made a face. "What's up with that, by the way? Are they fucking?"

"Get your mind out of the gutter. They're just friends. Ryan's straight."

Tristan raised his eyebrows. "You're supposedly straight, too, but it doesn't stop you from putting your cock in my body every day."

Zach pinched Tristan's buttock. "It's not your body. It's mine."

Tristan wasn't impressed in the least. He scowled, but before he could say anything, Zach tipped his face up and kissed him shortly. "This is my mouth, too," Zach said with an infuriating smirk.

"Fuck you," Tristan said before grabbing Zach's hair and pulling him into a deeper kiss. Zach moaned, his hand slipping into Tristan's trunks to cup his buttock, overconfident and proprietary as usual.

Someone catcalled. "My virgin eyes!"

Tristan tore his lips away and glared at Ryan, who was smirking at them from the pool. "Piss off, Ryan. And take your bleached shadow with you."

"I told you: I'm a natural blond," James said with a long-suffering look.

"He is," Ryan told Tristan, throwing an arm around his friend. "Come on, Jamie, prove it to Zach's boy." He hooked a finger on the waistband of James's trunks. "Take it off, show him."

"You're so gay," Tristan said. "And I'm not Zach's boy."

"Says the guy who moans my brother's name every night." Ryan grinned and said in a terrible imitation of Tristan's voice, "Oh yeah, Zach, harder—"

Tristan grabbed a Red Bull and threw it at his head, narrowly missing as Ryan ducked. "I don't sound like that!"

Zach—the traitor—was laughing. "You kinda do."

"I hate you," Tristan grumbled before glowering at Ryan. "Even if I am, you two are still gayer."

Ryan sighed, looking serious for once. "All right, it's getting kind of old. There's such a thing as friendship, you know. I mean, I love this git for some reason,"—he smirked when James elbowed him—"but even thinking of him that way grosses me out." He grimaced. "It would be like shagging a brother."

"Yup," James said. "Like shagging a twin. Gross. I mean, have you seen him naked?"

Grinning, Ryan gave James an obnoxiously loud kiss on the cheek. "I'm hot and you know it, babe."

James rolled his eyes and made a disgusted face. He wasn't pulling away, though.

Tristan wiggled his eyebrows. "Like shagging a twin? You guys ever heard of twincest?"

"You're a terrible person," Ryan said with a pinched look.

"Yep," James agreed.

"He is," Zach said with a laugh.

Tristan elbowed him in the ribs. Zach was supposed to be on his side!

"But he's my terrible person," Zach said, dropping a kiss on Tristan's head.

Tristan hid his face in Zach's shoulder. "You're turning into a sap."

"Aww," Ryan and James cooed in unison.

"Look at him!" Ryan teased. "He's blushing."

"Fuck off," Tristan muttered. "Am not."

"Yep, blushing," James said with a laugh. "He's totally sweet on you, Zach."

Tristan fidgeted. He was still far from comfortable talking about feelings in public.

"All right, that's enough," Zach said, a touch of steel appearing in his voice as he probably sensed Tristan's embarrassment and discomfort. His arm around Tristan tightened. "Leave him alone."

Tristan smiled, warmth spreading through his chest, wrapping and locking itself around his heart—still such a novel feeling but already very familiar. Zach was still an asshole and drove him crazy half of the time, but he *got* him. Zach knew when to tease, when to push, when to punish him for being a prick, when to give him space, and when to be stupidly overprotective. He got him.

Tristan waited until Ryan and James fucked off to the other end of the pool before looking at Zach. And for the first time he didn't mumble when he said the words, "I love you. I do."

The world didn't end.

Zach just looked at him for a moment before groaning with a frustrated look on his face.

Frowning, Tristan slapped him on the chest. "What is that supposed to mean?" Tristan was hardly an expert, but he was pretty sure that wasn't how people were supposed to react to love confessions.

"I can't take it when you're genuinely sweet and—" Zach shook his head with a laugh and leaned down to kiss him greedily. "Keep being my bitchy, grumpy little shit. Please. It's bad enough already."

Tristan smirked. "You do realize that now I'm going to be extra sweet just to drive you crazy, right?"

Zach sighed and kissed him again. "Brat," he said against his lips.

Tristan grinned. "Always."

The End

About the Author

Alessandra Hazard is the author of the bestselling MM romance series *Straight Guys* and *Calluvia's Royalty*.

Visit Alessandra's website to learn more about her books: http://www.alessandrahazard.com/books/

To be notified when Alessandra痴 new books become available, you can subscribe to her mailing list: http://www.alessandrahazard.com/subscribe/

You can contact the author at her website or email her at author@alessandrahazard.com.

Made in United States
North Haven, CT
20 June 2024

53870945R00139